AFTERBURN

(AFTER #1)

E. DAVIES

London Borough of Hackney	
91300001088360	
Askews & Holts	
AF ROM	£11.99
	6348591

Afterburn / E. Davies. – 1st ed.
ISBN: 978-1-912245-06-2

AFTERBURN

PROLOGUE

LIAM

"You've been a firefighter for nine years. Three of those have been with us here in Santa Barbara. By now, you know that your actions last night were beyond unacceptable."

Liam worked his jaw around as he stared at the ground. Shame flushed his cheeks, but the awkward knot in his chest wasn't just embarrassment at being told off by the chief. There was more.

Mostly, he wished he felt *more* guilty about what had kept him from getting to work on time. Or rather, *who*.

Fuck. He couldn't remember the guy's name. He kind of wished he could.

Then again...

"Lll—uhhh..."

Liam huffed out a quick laugh. "Liam." His skin tingled with heat as he curled his fingers into the warm back of a cotton t-shirt.

The man pressing his lips against Liam's neck snorted like he'd known that. "Of course." He laid one more open-

E. DAVIES

mouthed kiss on Liam's throat, then licked his way up to crush their lips together again.

Neither of them had, and that was fine by him.

"I'm not going to put it on your record."

That got Liam's attention. Last time, it had gone on his record in Santa Ana, and Boston before that. He was already doing the math on whether he could bid for a transfer and get in somewhere else... maybe somewhere with even better surfing. He could pick up surfing.

But Chief Williams wasn't putting it on his record? Why the hell not?

"I'm going to take a few days to think about this," Chief Williams continued like he didn't notice Liam's shock. "It's hard to find guys like you in this neck of the woods."

"I love your neck. It's so sensitive."

Liam moaned his appreciation and swayed on his feet in the middle of his living room, letting this gorgeous stranger kiss his way up his neck like he owned him. "Your lips are fuckin' great."

"Wanna feel them somewhere else?"

A shudder of desire ran straight from Liam's hot cheeks down his spine, hardening his cock as he pressed it into the stranger's thigh.

His lust made him shake from head to toe, his body flooded with adrenaline. One way or another, he had to find an outlet for it.

Really? Liam just followed the same informal code of conduct on the job that every other guy did. Plus, California was one of the hardest places to get a job in this field, because

2

everyone wanted to be here. Transferring here from Boston had been hell.

Chief Williams didn't want to replace him. Liam ignored the uncomfortable prickle of fear that this could be seen as... well, favoritism. After all, this was the only openly gay chief in California, and he was one of just a couple of openly gay people—three men and one woman—in the department.

"Oh." Liam couldn't think up anything else at the moment, and he didn't have to. Better not to talk back right now, especially if the chief was giving him a break.

"Everyone makes mistakes," Chief Williams told him, but his face was serious. Even if he wasn't putting it on the record, he was going to remember this. "But your actions put people in danger."

It hadn't been a catastrophic mistake; no calls had come in within those first two hours, before he'd checked his phone and found the string of calls and texts. Kevin had come to pick him up from the guy's house, and they'd made it back to the station before their first call had come in.

But it *could* have been. Especially this time of year; wildfires were starting to crop up, and their territory bordered on the Santa Barbara hills where they could sweep down, into the suburbs, without much notice. After the Jesusita and Tea fires, everyone was on high alert from March through October—and the season grew longer every summer.

Plus, their territory had all kinds of challenges: shopping malls, jam-packed residential neighborhoods, and wildland were the three big ones. All could be huge risks, especially if they were understaffed.

"I understand, sir," Liam said quietly. His throat was tight. He *knew* why it was wrong. Fuck, he did feel embarrassed when he focused on that.

But when he remembered his dick pressing into the tight-

3

ness of the hot little guy under him, the way the guy's body slammed into his with sharp groans, and best of all, the moment after orgasm when his shudders of arousal subsided into bone-melting bliss and dragged his eyelids shut...

Liam wasn't going to give that up. He'd gone three years without fucking up, even if he'd balanced on the line sometimes. He'd been on Grindr at work, he'd even sent videos and video chatted from the station bathroom, but he'd never crossed that line before now.

A guy had needs. If he had to transfer to escape scrutiny for another few years, he'd do it. If he *could*, that was.

Something told him Chief Williams wasn't going to let him go that easily.

"Head back to work. I'll catch you for a chat when I figure out what to do."

"Yes, sir." Liam rose to his feet and strode out of the office, ignoring the tension that knotted his shoulders. It was ironic: he needed another good fuck to get that tension out of his body.

1

DYLAN

One: bamboo. Two: reclaimed silk. Three: merino wool. Four: cotton. Five: the unmistakable fake feathery texture of acrylic.

Dylan recoiled, but he kept dragging his hand across the row of yarn skeins on the shelf, not caring that he disturbed some of them. They were brightly colored, each skewed stack of yarn a cluster of color against the plain shelf.

Now for things he saw. That was easy; he could pick out specific colors.

One: mulberry. Two: creamsicle. Three: dusky ocean. Four: whatever the hell that ugly salmon shade was called.

Dylan cracked a smile, the tremble in his hand subsiding as the clenched muscles in his shoulders gradually eased.

That was touch and sight, what senses were left? Dylan wracked his brain for a second before it came to him: he had to pin down three specific sounds.

The first sound was the squabble of girls' voices from the long table on the other side of the store. Chairs banged and shuffled across the floor. The third sound was his own hoarse breathing.

As the hairs on the back of his neck settled, Dylan closed his eyes, then wiped the cool sweat off his forehead with his wrist.

Two smells? Well, that was easy. The yarn section had its own scent—a thick, warm snarl of fibers. A second smell was the spiced cologne he'd dabbed on his wrists that morning for a quick escape when he needed one.

He only needed to name one taste. Birthday cake. The parents had insisted on serving cake *before* they arrived here for their craft session. They'd kindly brought slices in for the store staff—Dylan and his boss, Velma. It was a double-chocolate monstrosity with rainbow sprinkles, but he'd enjoyed it.

Oh, shit, the birthday party. Velma was probably considering drowning herself in sequins by now.

He wasn't sure how long he'd stepped away—a minute? Five? Time didn't exist when his brain slipped into fight-or-flight mode.

Through the stiff leather soles of his shoes, the solid-wood floorboards held Dylan upright, however much his knees felt like buckling. He turned his face toward the light streaming in through the giant glass windows that overlooked State Street.

He was here, and he was safe. *He* was the adult in charge.

Not that he felt like one yet. He was twenty-three—for years, he'd thought eighteen was the magic year; then it had become twenty-one. Now...

Dylan let out a quiet sigh. He had a job, and he needed to do it.

Steeling himself to deal with the brats again, he strode around the corner of the shelving, back to the tables in the middle of the shop. Usually, birthday parties went in the community and teaching room in the back. These parents had insisted on the craft shop atmosphere out here.

No sign of Velma, who was probably on another supply mission to the office.

For fuck's sake, weren't they done yet? The three boys who had come to pick up their sisters couldn't be more than thirteen. Christ, they were already Dylan's size, and had twice his most obnoxious attitude without even trying.

Their raised voices and stupid aggression had Dylan's heart racing ninety miles an hour. Worse yet, the ringleader was eyeing the hair of the girl next to him, a grin twisting his lips as he smeared glue across scraps of paper. The other two were grinning at Dylan, giving him the *whatcha gonna do?* look.

Honestly, Dylan didn't know. Sometimes, he thought the kids in this generation were no better than the ones who had made his own life hell.

He was panicking again, the air not quite filling his lungs no matter how deeply he tried to breathe. He couldn't bring himself to look over to the door as it jangled.

Kids were doing this to him? For fuck's sake, he was no better than them. But these kids weren't even technically here for the party, and the birthday kid's parents weren't around to supervise, so he couldn't threaten them with getting into trouble with an adult—

No, *he* was an adult! Why the fuck weren't they listening every time he told them to be quiet until the party was over?

But he heard a deep voice, not a bratty preteen's.

"Velma! Who do I call to get the shower fixed?"

Dylan managed to look over, then froze on the spot.

Shit. He was *gorgeous*.

Shirtless, the stranger wore dark blue jeans that rode low on his hips, his hair dark from water and pushed back. The water droplets trickling down his shoulders and across his ripped chest traced their way down his abs.

Dylan had never seen such a tightly-packed bundle of

muscles and nerves that still looked *sexy*. Not huge in a way that screamed *look at me*, but in the practical kind of way. The quiet way that screamed *I could pick you up and fuck you right up against this wall and not break a sweat.*

This was the upstairs tenant? Velma had told him the new tenant of the studio apartment above Green Door Crafts was a delicious firefighter, but he'd laughed it off.

He wasn't laughing now. Shit, she'd been telling the truth.

Best—or worst—of all, the guy had noticed him, and his face warmed up with a smile as he lowered his volume again.

"Oh. Hello."

No, that wasn't the best part. The best part was that the three bratty boys had gone dead silent.

Dylan tried to string words together. "Hey. Velma's, uh, in the office."

"Thank you." The guy hesitated for a moment, and Dylan didn't miss the quick flick of his eyes up and down his body.

The attention made him prickle with pleasure, heat flushing through his cheeks. He was already dizzy enough from these asshole kids, but having a man like this look at him like he was about to grade him?

He leaned hard on the nearest rack until the guy disappeared into the back.

Then, Cory or whatever his name was, the bratty ring-leader of the little group, started up again, approaching the table and grabbing the glue stick as he pushed his way between two of the girls at the craft table.

Dylan gritted his teeth. He wasn't sure they wouldn't just try to beat the shit out of him if he stopped them, but he had to try.

As soon as he approached, all three boys looked at him, puffing out their chests with all the reckless arrogance of kids who had no parents around to get them in trouble.

"What?" Cory demanded.

"You're not guests at this party. You're picking up Hannah and Lily, right?"

"Yeah? So?"

I bet they're horrible big brothers. Sorry, girls. Dylan glanced over at the two, who were engrossed in their scrapbook project, then back at the kids. "You can wait outside until they're done."

Just as he'd thought, Cory squared up to him, and he was already just an inch or two shorter than Dylan. "Nah, we don't want to."

"Yeah, it's hot outside. You can't make us. You work at a *craft store*," the second boy chimed in with a snicker. The third was keeping a lookout for Velma.

Dylan knew exactly how this was going to go.

This would end in pain.

His body was shutting down again, in anticipation.

Dylan froze on the spot, trying to tell himself that he was *not* going to lose his shit in front of them and give them the satisfaction.

"Maybe *he's* bound by his job to act polite toward little assholes like you, but *I'm* not."

Dylan smelled the guy's aftershave and shampoo and heard that deep voice booming from behind him before he saw him, but the guy swept past him in a few strides, his eyes narrow.

"Shut up and behave. If the nice man tells you to shut up and wait outside, you shut up and wait outside."

Dylan still couldn't move, his hands curled into tight fists. Heat pricked at the corners of his eyes as he focused on the ground under him, trying to go through his senses again—to find things around him to pull him out of this—but it was so fucking hard.

The only thing keeping him from losing it was the wall of

muscle between him and the three boys as the stranger bore down on them.

"Yeah." That was Cory, and it wasn't even his sarcastic voice. There was a note of genuine fear in there.

Who could blame him? This guy looked like he could toss all three boys out the window at the same time.

As the boys shuffled to the door, Dylan could have laughed —or cried—with relief.

He'd barely said a word to the guy, but he was already a heroic mythical bully-slayer in Dylan's eyes.

It wasn't just his size he was using to command respect, either. He had the kind of attitude that made all eyes turn to him—the girls distracted from their crafting, Velma as she emerged from the office and approached the table with supplies, and the ruffians he was confronting.

And Dylan, of course, whose cheeks burned with embarrassment and gratitude that he couldn't verbalize. Words weren't going to come out right now.

The door jangled, the boys went to hang out and kick the curb outside, and Liam turned to Velma. "Thanks, ma'am."

"No, thank you, Liam." Velma's eyes flickered to Dylan with concern. "I'll make sure that's fixed promptly."

"Great." Liam followed her gaze, then nodded once to her and turned to face Dylan again. "Hey."

Dylan, tongue-tied and frozen, just nodded slightly. That was all he could really manage, and his cheeks flushed with shame.

The broad, muscled body approaching blocked out Dylan's view of everything else, giving him a single point to focus on— please, God, his eyes and not his rippling, muscular chest. He was much closer, his voice lower and for Dylan's ears only.

Shit, he was just a foot away, and now there was a broad hand on his shoulder, jolting him back to attention.

"You okay?"

Dylan dragged his gaze up to those bright blue eyes that were focused on him as the guy pulled his hand back again. Did he look like he was in shock? The way Velma watched him, he had to look a mess.

"Y-Yeah. I... thanks," Dylan managed, but he didn't dare try full sentences.

Shit, he was *not* okay.

The stranger—this Liam—eyed him for a few seconds like he didn't believe him and was assessing his condition, but then nodded slightly and strode off again for the back stairs.

Dylan barely breathed. His shoulder still tingled with warmth where that broad hand had squeezed him, and he tried not to think about how much he ached to feel it again.

"Dylan, can you grab the spare glitter markers from the office?"

That was Velma, his boss. She had steel-gray hair that she'd earned through three iterations of this store. The first and second hadn't quite made it in the tough Santa Barbara craft market, but the third had stuck around.

Velma's eyes were a little *too* understanding.

Dylan winced as he nodded and made his escape to the office, his feet finally able to move from where he'd been rooted to the spot.

He tried his hardest not to panic about what she might say as he rummaged through the drawer of spare supplies for the glitter pens. Every raised voice from the shop outside made him flinch again, and his chest knotted with frustration at himself and the whole goddamn world.

Scraping his hands against the pencil leads in the basket made him pull them back, covering his face. "You... don't," Dylan hissed at himself, angrily pushing through the reflex and burying his fingers in the pens again.

As he'd expected, a minute later, Velma was knocking softly on the office door.

"I've got 'em." Dylan picked up a fistful of silver-, gold-, and copper-toned markers and brandished them in her direction, not meeting her eyes. "Non-toxic, in case the kids decide to color their tongues. Again."

"Dylan."

He had no choice but to look at Velma as he pushed himself away from the file cabinet. The tension in his chest eased when he saw no hint of pity in her eyes, and he straightened up, better able to look her in the face now. "Yep?"

"Wanna go home now, and supervise the knitting group this weekend instead?"

God, yes. Many weeks, Dylan attended the group anyway. Supervising was no problem. That just meant making sure nobody stole their stuff, helping teach newbies, and selling people knitting supplies now and then.

More importantly, he was so grateful for a way out right now that he could almost cry. Liam had rescued him from those little assholes, but he was still on edge. He still had a meltdown to get through, and he didn't want to do it in public.

Dylan's hands were shaking again, his breathing unsteady. "Yeah," he murmured, handing over the fistful of pens and rubbing his fist over his eyes. "I'm having... a day. I'm sorry."

He found kids hard to be around, but he wasn't usually this grumpy with them. He couldn't even hold down a goddamn job at a craft store without having a mental breakdown.

"It happens," Velma said. She knew him well enough not to squeeze his shoulder or pat his cheek like she sometimes did when he was feeling... normal. "And I could use the weekend off anyway."

She was trying to make Dylan feel better, but he let her. "Okay. Works for me. Thanks, Vee."

"No sweat, baby. See you tomorrow."

Dylan grabbed his car keys from the desk and let her bring the offering of glitter pens to appease the horde before sneaking out of the shop down the yarn aisle so he didn't have to look any of the kids in the eye. He kept his face turned well away from the three little brats waiting outside, but they didn't say a word anyway.

They were probably too scared of Liam coming back down the stairs and tossing them to the curb. That worked for Dylan. His pride could take that beating to save him from... well... a real beating.

The other problem, of course, was what to do when he got to the car. He wasn't always *able* to drive in this state. He'd tuned out before—lost whole chunks of his drive home. It scared the fuck out of him.

Luckily, he had a trick.

Once he was buckled in, Dylan started up his car, then pulled out of the lot with his hand resting on the top of the steering wheel. He pulled the lever on his seat to sit upright so he didn't have to lean forward when he reached behind the wheel with his other hand.

His fingers closed around his keys hard enough that the edges of his house, mailbox, and mom's house keys dug into his palm.

It wasn't painful, exactly, but it was attention-grabbing. He couldn't ignore the blunted bite, and it kept him in the moment. He pulled his other hand off the wheel to flick his turn signal.

"Almost home," he murmured, then fidgeted with the radio dial to turn it as far up as he could stand. With the LA traffic report blaring in his ear, he kept his mind on the road the whole way home.

2

DYLAN

"Don't let there be any snakes... don't let there be snakes..."

Stooped over a pile of brush, Dylan stared hard at the armful of dead grass he was scooping into his arms. Of all the outdoor chores Dylan least enjoyed, gathering up dead brush and grass was behind even lawn mowing.

If he had his way, he'd never let brush sit long enough to let snakes get uppity ideas about hiding places, but it wasn't his yard. This was his mom's place, and she couldn't seem to keep up with maintenance over the last few summers—since his dad died.

A stalk of grass wiggled just a *bit* too much.

Dylan squeaked and nearly dropped the whole armful, scrabbling backward a pace, but it was just a long blade of grass.

"Fucking hell," he muttered under his breath and hugged the armful closer to his chest as he straightened up and strode over to the wheelbarrow.

He had to man up and face this. Scrawny or not, he was still better-suited to this work than his mother. And if his mom realized that he was this worried about snakes, she'd insist he didn't do anything that bothered him. She'd leave the pile of brush back here to catch fire on some 110-degree day.

Here in the foothills, his parents—just his mom, Belle, now —had one of the more isolated properties. They backed onto wildland, which was great for avoiding neighbors, but more dangerous every summer. After the Jesusita and Tea fires, he'd once suggested moving, but his parents would never do that. They'd lived here for decades.

"Any fires nearby this season so far?" Dylan asked as his mom approached with a glass of lemonade. He wiped his forehead on his arm, pushing his hair back and taking the glass.

Even the ice-cold condensation on the outside of the glass was bliss. He rolled it carefully across his forehead before taking his first few gulps of the sugary, tart beverage.

"Two, but they didn't get close enough to be a real worry. Still... for this early in the season?"

Dylan shook his head. Even when he was a kid—which wasn't that long ago—fire season had only been a few months in the heat of the summer. But it started earlier now, ever since that damn drought. "That's crazy."

His mother hummed her agreement. "You don't have to do this, you know." She'd been trying to nudge him into relaxing and sitting around in her little oasis of a backyard, but he wasn't here to relax today.

"Oh, don't be silly. I need to be outside," he assured her. "Helps work out the stress."

"Is your coursework stressful? Your jobs?"

"Nah. I've only got one more exam before I have my associate's degree," Dylan told her. "The internship's not stressful, and the craft store's all right." He wasn't going to admit that he'd been a shivering mess yesterday.

"Do you need to have your stress grounded?"

"No, I've been grounding myself." Not in the way she meant, by visiting Darrell—the Reiki guy she'd taken him to as a kid. He'd stopped that after moving out. But he ate a lot of ice cream, which was basically the same thing.

He gulped down a few more sips of lemonade and surveyed the yard, hand on his hip.

It was typical desert landscaping—the only grass to mow was a small side yard. The rest was gravel and dirt garden beds, natural hills of hardy grasses and flowers, and a few trees. One huge tree overshadowed part of the yard, and raking up the leaves under it had been his first priority. Plus, everything needed pruning. These days, his mom only seemed to want to put together plant baskets and pots.

"Good. Darrell said he misses you, and said to say hello. I worry about you," she told him, squeezing his arm.

"Hi back to him." He offered her a quick smile. "I'm fine, Mom."

Belle looked doubtful, but she nodded. "What year are you in, then, technically? I can never keep it straight."

"Er... I'm kind of a sophomore and a half," Dylan laughed. He was a nontraditional student, finishing a few last classes at the city college before he transferred. That was another of his failures he didn't want to think about.

The thought of tuition at the university here as opposed to the city college made his heart race, but he'd spent the last two-plus years working through a little over a year's worth of course-work so that his grades would be higher and he'd qualify for scholarships.

He was going to be fine, financially. Socially? God only knew. At a university that size, with classes that size, he might just flunk out again. God, he felt totally lost sometimes. He was barely an adult, and worse yet, he didn't have anyone to ask about how to do important things like not fail at life.

"Oh, that reminds me. They sent me my credit card bill late *again*," Dylan frowned. There was no use asking his mom what to do about it—she didn't believe in credit except maybe from community-centric lenders with carbon-neutral offices. But he could at least vent.

She made a sympathetic noise. "I keep telling you, I can help you get off the grid. You don't even have to move back home. A nice little studio up here in the hills for you to practice from, someday..."

At least she was proud of him for his eventual career goal: a master's in art therapy. It was just barely hippie-approved, since he wasn't going to prescribe any mind-altering drugs. It made him laugh sometimes that she'd have less trouble with him prescribing unlicensed mind-altering drugs.

"I'll think about it," he fended off her inquiry with a laugh and handed back the empty glass. "Thanks, Mom."

"Of course, sweetie. Come sit down after you're done with that pile." She headed back into the shade to sit at the picnic table and continue her crossword.

Dylan smiled. "Yeah, will do." His strength renewed, he grabbed his trusty rake to poke the rest of the pile before he dumped it into the wheelbarrow. Bit by bit, the yard was looking nicer.

There were a few minutes of silence before she spoke up again. "You know, that Allen boy, Kai, is back out here."

She was hitting all her usual motherly points today: emphasizing self-care through dubious medical procedures, encouraging him to opt out of the real world and become a hippie, and now trying to set him up with a nice doctor.

"He's living with his parents again, now that med school is over. I think he's on a placement at some teaching hospital."

17

"Is he?" Dylan answered, wheeling the barrow toward the side yard. With that pile cleared, he just had to prune some of the dead growth back and the yard would look fresh and tidy.

"You should go over and say hello. I can call Cindy and get his schedule."

He really didn't need his mom and Kai's mom conspiring to get them together. They'd grown up in the same neighborhood, two of the only openly gay boys even out here in liberal California. Kai had been one of the few kids who'd missed him at school after his parents had pulled him out to finish his schooling at home. Of course they'd been friends... and then more.

As far as he knew, neither set of parents had ever found out about them dating for a hot second before Kai had realized that he didn't want to be with a fem guy like Dylan. It might have tarnished his cool surfer boy reputation or something.

Dylan didn't resent him for having preferences, but he did wish he hadn't tested them out on him. A perfectly good friendship, gone in one summer. And there wouldn't be a second chance. That was the one thing he did right: he didn't make romantic mistakes twice.

"Right," Dylan absently answered. "Maybe."

For once, his mother didn't push it. She looked over her paper at him for a minute, then back down to it to keep doing her crossword.

As he silently yanked the last of the dead plants out of the ground and hopped out of the back garden bed, Dylan sighed. It could be worse. It had always been this way: his mom didn't always know what to do with him, but at least she tried.

On the way by, Dylan leaned down and half-hugged her. "Thanks, Mom."

He got that spaced-out smile in return that meant she

didn't know how to respond, and a little pat on the back. "Take care of yourself."

"I'll be fine."

In reality, Dylan was relieved she dropped the subject so easily. The last thing he needed right now was love.

3

LIAM

Driving to the station on a day off, dressed in his fire station t-shirt and jeans, was weird. His work uniform was a cool long-sleeved shirt and pants specially designed to keep from melting under his turnout gear. Going to the house in anything other than that made his stomach tight with anxiety, because his brain knew something was up.

Chief Williams had told him to come in after his shift was over and he'd slept. It was a good call. Now that he was fresher, rested, and clean—even if he'd only gotten to have a cold shower—he felt ready to face the music.

Sort of.

He managed to avoid running into anyone until he got to the chief's office.

"Like I said yesterday, this is all off the record."

Chief Williams's first words took Liam aback all over again. He crinkled his brow but nodded, running a hand back through his hair.

"All right."

"This isn't an order, but a bit of... call it friendly advice. I'd like to see you get into therapy."

Liam's jaw dropped with surprise and... well, amusement.

Sure, he'd run into his share of suicides, DOS incidents, torn-up families, and the works, but no major incident. No roof collapses with coworkers inside, no near-death experiences where he flashed out of his body or anything like that.

Certainly nothing to be depressed or traumatized by beyond the post-incident reviews they all conducted. Chief Williams was careful to make sure they didn't bring that shit home more than they had to.

So why single him out?

"Er... if you don't mind my asking..." Liam started, trying not to word it like he was talking back.

Chief Williams nodded slightly. "Why?"

"Yeah."

"Let me just say I've noticed certain patterns of behavior, and I worry, because I've been there, too."

"Ah." From anyone else, Liam would fear the chief was trying to get him to conversion therapy or something fucked-up like that. This was almost the opposite, and it made Liam smile.

Did he think he'd been in some bad relationship or something? That he was missing work because of some jealous ex-boyfriend, or new fling?

Mostly, Liam wanted the conversation to be over. It made him uncomfortable on a level he wasn't really prepared to confront. "Okay."

"All right? Start working on finding something that works for you and let me know when you do."

"Yes, sir."

Liam rose to his feet, his mind already working.

Of course, he had no plans of seeking out therapy for some problem that didn't really exist. His fondness of hookups was nothing to be ashamed of, even if the details were sketchy sometimes. It was forgetfulness that had made him miss work.

At least it wasn't on his record. If he transferred, he could start afresh—again. It was a pain in the ass learning new territory and getting seniority all over again, but whatever. He could deal with that.

He *did* need a little stress relief, though, and he had a pretty good idea where to find it.

The craft store Liam lived over, Green Door, was a cute little place. Not being a DIY fan, crafts geek, or manly scarf knitter himself, Liam had rarely popped in, except to visit Velma.

He wouldn't mind bouncing his choice—whether to get therapy he didn't really need or transfer to a place he didn't want to move to—off her. She seemed like the no-bullshit type, from his brief conversations with her, and she had no personal investment in the issue like his own parents might.

And if she was out, that meant the hot little guy with the pretty green eyes would be in. Liam wouldn't complain about bumping into him—preferably naked and repeatedly.

Win-win.

As soon as he parked in his usual side-street spot, Liam grinned. He recognized the cute little blue beater car parked in front of his. By now, he'd seen it enough to figure it was an employee's car. Velma didn't have a car, which meant Dylan was in.

Liam headed for the door to the store instead of the stairs.

"Welcome—oh."

Even yesterday, sleep-deprived and damp from his shower, distracted by the asshole kids who wouldn't shut up, Liam had noticed how fucking cute Dylan was.

He was a couple inches shorter, but he stood straight and swished a little when he walked. He had that kind of bright gay air about him that was impossible to miss.

Liam could pass as straight if he wanted, but this guy? Not a chance.

It made him grin, really, as did the way Dylan's cheeks turned pink.

Poor guy had been outnumbered by the three kids probably half his age, but all of his size. It had clearly been embarrassing to accept Liam's help shooing them off, and near the end... well, he'd looked outright panicky. Liam hoped he didn't associate his presence with bad things now.

"Hey," he greeted.

"Hi again." Dylan's voice was light and shy as Liam looked him up and down, taking in his work uniform—a polo shirt with the Green Door logo and dark pants.

"Hard at work again?" Liam asked, grinning at the way Dylan had to crane his neck up to look at him. A quick glance around showed the craft shop empty—no surprise, at eleven on a Thursday. "You work full time here?"

"No. I mean, yes to the first, no to the second. It's not much work... right now... but it can be. Part-time."

Oh, man. He's cute. Watching Dylan get all flustered as he tried not to stare at the fire department logo on his chest made Liam tingle with pleasure. "Oh," he teased, his grin still firmly in place. He winked. "What time do you get off, then?"

Dylan's cheeks flushed. He didn't miss the implications. "Not until this evening."

"Oh," Liam frowned sympathetically—and, he wasn't gonna lie to himself, with a little disappointment. He didn't want to wait a few hours for this guy to change his mind or get shy. "Well, I live right upstairs..." He wasn't even subtly making a pass.

"So I gathered," Dylan responded, and he was grinning back now. "But is your shower fixed?"

"Not until tomorrow."

"Mmmm," Dylan hummed as he leaned against the yarn shelf, one hand on his hip. "I dunno, then. Might be safer to chat down here. And my name's Dylan, by the way, in case you wanted to know." His head was tilted slightly, his eyes sparkling.

Liam laughed. It was so much better to see him looking like this, not like he was about to pass out. "Hi. I'm Liam, and I've got four days off and nothing planned, so..."

"Yeah?" Dylan looked interested. "You're a firefighter? Or is that just for a costume party?"

Liam laughed again at how fucking cheeky this guy was. It was a playful sense of humor that made him stand to attention. "I'm not just roleplaying, although I can do that, too," he teased. "If you're into that."

"I'll remember that." Dylan slid his hands into his pockets, and he wasn't looking away now. Those rosy cheeks were dimpled. "Which station, then?"

"Four. This area isn't part of my territory, actually," Liam told him. As sexy as it would be to be the protector of Dylan's store, he'd thought it best to live a little outside his own territory. He liked it downtown where he could walk to the pier and eat out at different restaurants every day. "See?" He pointed at the logo on his chest.

That gave Dylan an excuse to push away from the shelves and lean in to look at his chest, and Liam didn't miss that Dylan's eyes caught the hard nubs of his nipples poking at his t-shirt.

His body would fit perfectly against Liam's.

"Protectors of the north side? Sounds important." Dylan stepped back again so he could make better eye contact. "The hours must be brutal, though. I don't know a lot," he confessed, but his eyes were sparkling with interest in Liam.

And unless Liam was mistaken, that was genuine interest in the job, not just the shallow interest that served as an excuse to get closer to him.

Liam had almost forgotten how good it felt to chat without the pressure of wondering when they'd make out, already.

Not that he didn't want that, but he wasn't going to get Dylan into trouble in his own workplace after getting himself into trouble just two days ago.

"It can be stressful," Liam agreed. "Makes it hard to date." *Not that I care about that.* That went unsaid. "What about you? Part-time here...?"

"And part-time at a co-op internship at a therapy office," Dylan supplied. "And part-time student."

"Jesus." Liam had already been a little interested in what a cute young guy like him was doing with himself to be working at a craft store, but suddenly, Dylan was much more interesting. "What are you doing all that for?"

"I'm in psych, planning to specialize in art therapy."

"Ahhh." Liam wasn't sure he'd ever run into someone quite like Dylan, even in these couple of minutes of chatting. "Wow."

For a moment, Dylan looked embarrassed. He rubbed his forehead and shrugged, a sudden vulnerability in his eyes. "I dunno. I've been taking it slow getting to this point. I'm twenty-three and I'm not even done with my BA."

"I'm twenty-seven and so far, the BS hasn't stopped," Liam countered with a grin. "That's life. You're doing good to have a career path already."

Dylan laughed, his shoulders sinking again with relief. "Thanks. It was sort of an accident. I just wound up getting this job at the same time as starting my degree, and then... it clicked into place."

"Oh." Now that Liam was thinking with his upstairs brain, Dylan was somehow even more interesting. "What makes you want to be a therapist? I mean, you're going to hear so much... bad stuff, right?"

"What makes you want to fight fires?" Dylan countered immediately, smiling.

Oof. He doesn't pull his punches. "Fair enough," Liam said with a laugh. "Yeah, we do see bad stuff, but... I never thought of doing anything else. Got my first firefighting job at eighteen, and it just stuck."

"I saw my first therapist at thirteen, so," Dylan rolled his eyes with a self-deprecating smile. "Pretty much the same."

Liam didn't want to push at that point. There was something making Dylan's smile tighter, and his heart throbbed with fear about what that could be. He had a few ideas. Not a lot of thirteen-year-olds wound up in therapy. "Oh. So you wanted to get into art therapy right away?"

"No, I hated therapy," Dylan told him with a quick, sharp laugh. "It was pretty recent when I realized it didn't have to be shitty."

"Ohhh." Liam grimaced. "Yeah, my chief actually..." *What the fuck? Why am I telling him this?* But it just felt right. There was something strange and tentative building between him and this stranger.

Maybe it was because he had nothing left to lose. He could just trade jobs with some guy living in a shittier city. Other guys would jump at the chance to be here in Santa Barbara.

Or maybe it was Dylan's warm gaze fixed on him like he was the most interesting person in the world—not just the hottest and most available that happened to be in the room.

Liam wasn't used to being watched like this.

"Yeah?" Dylan prompted.

To hell with it. "My chief wanted me to get some kind of

support. I guess 'cause it's a stressful job," Liam lied. He wasn't going to tell Dylan he'd been failing at the one thing he always got right—his job.

Dylan lit up like he saw his chance to be helpful. "Ohhh. My clinic is really nice. The Green Tree, on the corner of State near that fire station. I don't know if that's your station or not. But there's also support groups, and... sorry." Dylan broke off, looking embarrassed. "I won't go community resource encyclopedia on you."

Liam was already laughing. Dylan had lunged to talk about his field of expertise, and it was adorable. "No, go on."

"There's all kinds of support circles. Depression, anxiety, PTSD, general stress. Mindfulness meditation, yoga, you name it. We have a knitting circle here for people with PTSD. A surprising number of guys go here, actually." Dylan glowed with pride. "It was my idea to host it here."

"A knitting circle? For men?"

"For everyone, but it wound up being mostly guys right now," Dylan told him. "We have some ex-military vet types, some younger guys who work in uniform services, a lot of civilians with all kinds of traumas. I go, a lot." He shifted for a second, his eyes flickering away and then back to Liam like he was nervous he'd judge him.

Oh, cutie. Last thing I'd do is judge you. On the contrary, Liam respected Dylan for being man enough to admit to having mental health issues on their very first proper meeting. Not a lot of guys would admit to it, even after a major on-the-job incident.

"Good for you." Liam's mind was turning this over. If he told the chief he had a support group of some kind as he stayed around here... would he let it go?

He didn't know when he'd shifted to thinking *if I stay* to

I'm staying, but it had been during this conversation with Dylan. That was enough to catch him way off-guard.

The door rattled, making Liam almost jump. He'd been so engrossed in the conversation that he'd barely remembered they were still in Dylan's workplace.

"I'd better—"

"Yeah, of course!" Liam had to head upstairs sooner or later, even if Dylan wasn't joining him. "I'll see you in a bit. Better get lunch."

As Dylan gave him one more shy smile and nod, he strode off to greet the latest customer.

Liam let out a breath as he headed for the back stairs. He was genuinely interested in this guy—his cheeky smile, the flashes of brutal, even self-deprecating honesty that shone through... Dylan was the opposite of the fake, shallow types he usually let flock to him. And Dylan wasn't flocking—he was even resisting. That intrigued Liam even more.

Was Dylan his type? He could stick around long enough to find out.

28

4

DYLAN

The room was almost empty, but as Dylan hunched over the paper, he ignored the steady stream of students leaving the exam early.

This was his last exam. His last chance to boost his grades, and with a quarter of his final mark for the class depending on how he did right now, he was *not* wasting the chance to look over his answers one last time.

As he slowly reread his essay, checking for syntax errors, he frowned with annoyance and sheltered himself from the view of the aisle with his hand. The professor was scribbling the minutes left on the whiteboard for the benefit of students who didn't think to bring watches.

He was carefully detached from his personal feelings about the essay he'd written. The question was on how children's memories of trauma would differ based on their age.

Toddlers are unlikely to remember recurring traumatic events, unless they deviate greatly from the norm. Ongoing abuses are likely to blur into a haze of memory, while they may remember a one-time assault or some form of abuse that was significantly more impactful.

He hated that word, impactful, but he couldn't think of a better way to phrase it without erasing and rewriting the whole paragraph.

This class ought to have been easy, and in some ways, it was. He didn't need a teacher to tell him how an eleven-year-old would cope with trauma. He'd barely studied that module. Not because of avoidance, he tried to persuade himself, but the review of PTSD had shaken that belief.

It was useful stuff to know, but God, he'd be glad not to face this class twice a week every week. He was positive it wasn't good for his own mental health to constantly compare his own symptoms and experiences to the textbooks.

Then again, he suspected half of the psychology students in his class were in the degree because they were somehow fucked-up and wanted to learn more. The others were like vultures or spectators at a zoo, acting fascinated by all the "weird shit" people did without seemingly noticing that their own classmates were those people.

He was barely going to have time to grab coffee before heading to work at the clinic if he didn't hurry up. With these thoughts, Dylan was too distracted to properly proof his essay. It would have to stand as it was. He pushed himself to his feet and strode to the front of the classroom to hand in his paper.

The classroom door clicked shut behind him before he let himself pump his fist in victory, then dug out his phone from his pocket.

"Aw, shit."

It was almost eleven. He'd been in there until pretty much the last minute anyway. The bright side was that waiting until later to grab his Starbucks meant the breakfast lineup was over and the lunch rush hadn't started yet. He breezed through the drive-through on his way to open the clinic.

He juggled the coffee cup and the steering wheel, trying to down a little of the scorching liquid to wake him up again. Fucking 8 a.m. exams.

He liked to get into work fifteen minutes early so the clinic doors were open good and early before the first scheduled appointment. Hopefully Gary's first patient of the day would be the late type.

By the time he found parking alongside the clinic and juggled his coffee around to lock up the car, he caught sight of someone leaning against the side of the building, waiting for him to unlock the doors.

A second glance made him stop in his tracks. "Shit," he whispered.

It was Liam.

Of course it was the firefighter who had flirted with him to help him kill that boring afternoon... whose eyes had undressed him several times over, whose invitation up to his apartment had been barely veiled under conversation...

And who was a total hottie hunk.

Even now, as he leaned against the side of the building, his thumbs hooked into his jeans pocket, the fire station t-shirt stretching tight across his barrel chest and around his wide biceps, Liam looked *gorgeous*.

Embarrassed heat rose to Dylan's cheeks as he trotted up to the clinic door and Liam glanced over to take him in, pushing himself away from the building with a grin. "Morning. Sorry to keep you waiting."

Liam's slow smile and sparkling eyes made a chill run down Dylan's spine despite the stifling heat that was crawling over the city now that the morning fog had lifted. "It's no problem. I wondered if I'd see you today."

"I'm glad you came here! I mean, not that I'm pressuring you to come here," Dylan hastily added, in case Liam thought he was judging him for his obvious reluctance to be here. Standing next to Liam, fumbling with the clinic keys, was making his spine prickle with pleasure. He tried to ignore the itch under his skin to lean into him. Liam was a little taller, a little broader... exactly the type he wanted spooning him.

"No, I know."

"Gary's a great therapist." He turned the keys in the lock and pushed his hip into the door to open it. At the same time, tipped the cup in his other hand a little too far. He poured coffee across the back of his hand and the floor. "Oh, shit!" It wasn't scorching anymore, but it was hot enough to leave a painful sting for a moment.

Before he could take another breath, Liam pulled his slender hand into his body, raising his t-shirt to pat the coffee off. "How hot is it?"

Dylan caught his breath. The friction of his palm sliding against Liam's made his body flush with heat, and with Liam's t-shirt up...

Holy shit, did he have abs.

Dylan was blushing furiously now, but he didn't want to pull his hand back. "Not that bad. It's not too burny."

"Run it under cold water, just to be safe," Liam advised him, frown lines creasing his forehead. In that split second, he'd changed from teasing flirtation to the sweetest worry over him.

Dylan hardly knew how to handle the attention as he stepped into the lobby and Liam finally let go of his hand. *Damn it. I kind of wanted him to keep holding it.* "Thanks," he mumbled and headed straight for the staff room to run cool water over his hand as heat prickled under his skin.

Liam leaned in the doorway and watched him. "It didn't look like a bad one."

"No, just a little scalding to wake me up," Dylan laughed sheepishly. The cool water felt good, at least. He glanced down his front to make sure he hadn't poured it on his clothes, though he hadn't felt a sting. "It's my fault for being late and in a rush."

"That doesn't..." Liam trailed off, then rolled his eyes and laughed. "Why were you rushing?"

Dylan turned off the water and gently patted his hand dry. His skin didn't look too bad—a little red, but not blistered. "Just finished writing my last exam in a course. Actually in my associate degree."

"Holy shit!" Liam straightened up, looking impressed, and Dylan's chest glowed with pride. "Great work."

"Thanks." Dylan approached Liam, who stepped aside for him, and his shoulder brushed Liam's chest on the way past. It made him shiver with delight. "I should get you properly checked in. Gary prefers to do the intake assessment himself by talking to you, so there isn't much paperwork, but I'll need your name and address, that kind of stuff, once I get the computer started up."

Liam shrugged his agreement and came to lean on the counter instead.

He was so distracting, just standing there in his hot, tight t-shirt. Dylan had to try desperately to keep himself from flirting more. "Gary should be here any minute now..."

"I'll get all the hitting on you out of the way with now," Liam promised, a roguish twinkle in his eye.

Dylan's cheeks were warm as he sank into his chair and grinned up at Liam. "Very considerate."

"What's a smart guy like you doing after his associate's? Going right into... you said art therapy?"

Liam seemed genuinely interested in him, so Dylan leaned back and smiled as he waited for his computer to start up. "Thanks," he chuckled. "Um, no, it's a long road to go. This is a co-op position, but I still need to transfer to a state university for the rest of my undergrad BA, and then a master's, at the very least."

Liam whistled. "That sounds like a pain in the ass."

"It will be, but... like I said, I always wanted it."

"I'm proud of you—sorry, that sounds weird," Liam laughed. "But I'm glad for you that you figured out what you want and you're going for it. That's commendable."

Dylan couldn't stop smiling. It didn't sound weird to him at all. He could count on one hand the people who were proud of him for his career ambitions. "Most people go, '*Uh, art therapy? Have you thought of psychiatry?*'" he rolled his eyes. "Which I have, but my mom would kill me."

"Why?" Liam laughed.

"For going to the dark side. Big Pharma." Dylan gave Liam an easygoing smile. "Right, I'll need your details."

Liam's last name was Knight, which seemed oddly appropriate for a protector of the town. Dylan resisted the urge to take down his phone number for himself. Patient privacy.

At least, until Liam leaned over the counter and murmured, "Can I ask for yours? I'd normally wait until you're not at work, but it seems like all I do is run into you at work."

"Y-Yeah," Dylan laughed and told Liam his number. Just in time, too—as Liam put his phone back in his pocket, his boss, Gary, walked in.

Gary was one of two practitioners here. He co-owned the place with an older woman who reminded Dylan of his mom, but she hadn't been here a lot lately. She also practiced out of another clinic across town with fancier clients. Gary was just here, and he was easier to work for. He'd talked a lot with Dylan in quiet hours and empty appointment slots about therapy as a career since his co-op placement began.

"Morning, Dylan. Hello," Gary introduced himself to Liam with a handshake. "I'm Gary. I'll be your therapist today."

"Thanks. Great to meet you. Liam."

Gary looked over at him, then his office. "Dylan, have you finished with registration?"

"Yep." Dylan saved Liam's profile. Normally he'd be long finished with that, and Liam would have had a few minutes to unwind with a cup of water or coffee. When he cast Liam a quick glance of apology, Liam just smiled back.

"If you'd like to come on in," Gary welcomed Liam into the office.

When the door clicked shut, Dylan let out a breath he hadn't realized he was holding.

Every time Liam was in the room, he was all he could concentrate on. He hadn't even remembered to clean up the coffee spill. He grabbed a paper towel to mop up the liquid and grabbed his half-full cup from the table near the entrance. The memory of his clumsiness was embarrassing, sure, but it was totally worth it to have Liam hold his hand for those few seconds.

Just like Liam had swooped in to rescue him from those brats at the craft shop, he'd been right there, his eyes concerned and protective. Was that part of his job, or was that the kind of guy he was?

It would probably be a bad idea to plan another accident to find out. Fine. He'd get to know Liam the old-fashioned way—drawn-out flirting in person and over texts.

He'd only talked to the guy three times, but Dylan hadn't been so excited about that idea in ages.

5

LIAM

"So, the bad news or the bad news?"

Gary's tone was friendly and he was smiling, which kept Liam relaxed. He leaned back in the comfortable stuffed chair, his hands folded in his lap.

It had been a fine appointment—he'd explained that he didn't really feel anything was wrong, admitted to Gary with a little embarrassment—but mutual amusement—what had gone wrong to land him here, and described his daily life.

There was nothing to be worried about.

"The bad news, I suppose," Liam shrugged.

"I have a waitlist of a few weeks for all but the most urgent cases," Gary told him. "And given what we've just discussed," he gestured, open-palmed, "I don't think you'd qualify."

Liam was shaking his head before Gary even finished talking. "God, no." He wasn't going to take a spot from someone who actually needed one.

"In the meantime, to satisfy your chief's requirement for some kind of program, can I suggest finding a group? I can help connect you with support circles and groups in the area. I think a trauma support group is the way to go. Even if no individual work incident seems to be at fault here, the stress-relief and coping mechanisms you'd learn there could benefit you."

That made sense to Liam. "Yeah. That's perfect." In fact, he had an idea where he could find said group. "Actually... Dylan was mentioning... a knitting circle at his store."

Gary paused, then laughed. "Yes. I was actually going to ask how you felt about knitting."

"I honestly haven't thought about it," Liam laughed. He wasn't ashamed of it, but he'd never hear the end of it from his buddies at the house if they found out about him going to this kind of thing. They never had to, though. It was just down the stairs from his apartment, after all. Easiest thing in the world. "I'll try it."

"Good man," Gary praised and reached out for a hand-shake as they rose to their feet. "It was a pleasure to meet you, Liam. Dylan will be in touch when I have an available appointment slot—or, hopefully, Chief Williams accepts your support group involvement. Stay out of trouble," he added with a smile as they walked to the office door.

"I'll try," Liam laughed sheepishly. No more going home with guys right before a shift, that was for sure.

When they emerged into the reception, there was someone else waiting in the lobby with a magazine, shuffling her feet and looking nervous. Gary stopped for a word with Dylan before he headed over to greet her.

Liam ambled to the front desk and smiled. "Hi."

"Hey," Dylan smiled. "So, your insurance was billed fine, we shouldn't need anything else from you. Gary said you're looking for information on that knitting group?"

"I thought I'd give it a shot," Liam shrugged. "My chief should be cool with it."

"Great. You just missed one, but it's Wednesday evenings

from seven onward. The store closes at seven, but we leave the door open—though you can take the back stairs, I suppose."

The staircase that led up to his apartment connected to the store through a tiny, little-used side door. Sometimes he took it when he needed to talk to Velma about something in the apartment. Honestly, now and then he popped down to see her just for company. She always had something new and interesting in stock.

"Okay. I can do Wednesdays," Liam nodded. He had Dylan's number, more importantly, so he doubted it would be that long before they talked to each other. "I better get going, but I'll see you soon, huh?" he winked.

Dylan's cheeks were adorably rosy and round as he smiled back. "Yeah, see you soon."

Liam walked with a spring in his step as he walked to his car. He ignored the part of him that wondered what the hell he was doing trying arts and crafts just to get laid.

It wasn't *just* to get laid. After all, as much as Dylan flirted, Liam had offered straight-up sex and Dylan had neatly avoided his offer. Maybe he wanted to be romanced. But all that was beside the point. Liam had to do it for work reasons; Dylan just happened to be involved, and that sweetened the pot.

He wasn't missing Wednesday evening for the world.

6

DYLAN

"Then you move that needle that way, and slide this through that loop..."

Liam's eyes were narrowed, the knitting almost up by his nose as he squinted at the pattern of interlocking loops that made up his dishcloth.

Dylan was glad he'd started him on an easy project. He wasn't even getting him to purl around the edge to keep it flat yet. A square of curly knitted fabric was good enough for an absolute beginner.

Liam's hands were surprisingly delicate, but he was gripping the needles way too tight.

Resisting the temptation to lean in further, Dylan tapped his wrist. "Loose hands," he reminded him for the fifth or sixth time in an hour.

"Oh, God," Liam groaned and relaxed his hold. He had to fight the needle for the rest of the row, but his next row loosened up, at least. The fabric pinched in for a row or two and relaxed for a row or two, marking the patterns of his stress. "I can't stop doing that."

"You can," Dylan smiled. He leaned back on two legs, glancing around the rest of the group. They hadn't gotten to the support bit yet, since there were a couple of newcomers: Liam and one other woman who was being coached by Velma. They spent the first half-hour shooting the shit, buying supplies if necessary, and knitting. Then conversation usually began, guided by Jonathan.

Jonathan was a young therapist who'd only been practicing for a couple of years. He'd started off wanting to do art therapy for people with PTSD, but at the last minute, he'd chosen EMDR—eye movement desensitization and reprocessing—as his specialty. This was his *pro bono* service. It was something he could offer clients who couldn't afford his rates. The community project had come a long way in the last six months.

"Do we have most of our regulars around?" That was Jon, his expression relaxed and arms folded. "Yeah? How are our newbies doing?"

"I think I've got the hang of it," Liam answered, though he didn't raise his eyes from his needles as he carefully slid stitches from one needle to the other.

The other newcomer laughed, looking embarrassed. "A little slower than him to catch on."

"Oh, heaven, no," Velma clicked her tongue. "Rome wasn't built in a day. I'll pick up any stitches you slip."

"Are we ready to chat about the week?"

Dylan settled back with his own knitting—a silk scarf using gorgeous reclaimed yarn made from saris. He'd been working slowly on the project for a few weeks now, but he wanted to finish it tonight. It was only a short one, meant for fashion rather than warmth; it wasn't like he needed warmth in the Santa Barbara winters, after all.

As conversation went around the table, everyone said as

much or as little as they wanted about their week. Some people just said it was a bad one, while a few people went into detail.

Dylan loved this. He got to see snippets of people's lives unfold, week by week. They'd watched one guy get ready to propose successfully to his girlfriend, another woman recover from a car accident, and best of all, they'd seen people learn and teach each other coping strategies to get through the week.

Jonathan tried to direct conversation everywhere but the newbies, letting them see everyone else's varied ways of answering before they felt pressured to share anything about themselves.

When it was finally Liam's turn, Dylan kept his eyes on the scarf so Liam would have one less pair of eyes making him nervous, if he was the type to be nervous about public speaking.

Liam's voice was strong, though. "I'm a firefighter. I actually live right above this shop." A murmur of interest went through the group. "Yeah. I'm just here because my chief thinks I need more social support. Uh, I feel honored to be around you all. You all have so many stories. I don't know if I'm as interesting to be around, but it's great to be here. Thanks for sharing."

Was there something he wasn't telling me, or is he really wondering why he's here? Either way, Dylan would make sure he felt welcome to come downstairs

"Thanks for being here," Jonathan answered. "We don't require anyone to talk about their life stories. Just coming out is enough."

Liam snorted with amusement. "Oh, I did that years ago."

A ripple of laughter went through the room, and Dylan grinned at his scarf. Ballsy move, considering how many of the guys here were vets and cops. He must not have been closeted, then.

That made him relax. Not that he minded closeted guys, but he hated being asked to be discreet when they hung out.

Er, assuming they were going to hang out. Dylan scolded himself for his assumption, his cheeks hot. Liam had been interested in sex, but that didn't mean he wanted friendship, or friends-with-benefits, or whatever they wound up becoming.

They'd texted a little that week, but the flirting was at a low simmer. Dylan certainly hadn't gazed at the door to the stairs and wondered if he should pop upstairs after work sometime.

"Thank you for sharing," Jonathan smiled as Liam looked back down at his knitting to focus on finishing the row.

Their group exercise that day was talking about triggers—what they were, how to recognize them, and some common examples. Since the group had a mix of people who came and went, sometimes topics were repeated, and this was one Dylan recognized. It was still helpful to refresh the basics, though.

The usual examples came out: loud noises like fireworks, crowds, helicopters, or trash in the street. Those were the kinds of things veterans usually said. It didn't take long before others were speaking up, though, prompted by Jonathan. Dancing closely in clubs, abruptly braking in vehicles, or hearing about others' family members were other suggestions.

Liam didn't speak up at all, but he curiously listened as he worked his way through the square Dylan had given him to knit. "For firefighters, would something like fire do it? I don't know if I know anyone with PTSD at the station, but... wouldn't that be a problem?"

"If a firefighter experienced a fire-based trauma, yes, it could be that simple," Jonathan nodded. "But it's treatable, too. There are other possible triggers, too. Can you give me an example of a traumatic incident?"

Liam opened his mouth, glanced around the group, and

seemed to change his mind on what he was going to say. "A large-scale fire, like a mall. Those are really dangerous."

"Right. So, obviously, going to the mall could be a trigger for that person," Jonathan answered. "Anyone else?"

"Open areas, or big buildings," the police officer who'd been coming every few weeks suggested.

"The time of day, or something that was going on right before you got the call."

Liam's brows rose. "Ohhh. Yeah. I get it."

"That's a good example, actually. Triggers aren't always the exact situation the individual was in," Jonathan explained, looking around the group. "They can seem totally unrelated to someone else who wasn't there. If you couldn't save someone in a mall fire in, say, a toy store... teddy bears could be triggering."

Liam nodded. "Thanks. Sorry. They don't give us any kind of training on this."

"No, no. It's good you asked," Jonathan assured him, and Dylan nodded. It was so easy for Dylan to forget that a lot of people had zero knowledge on the subject at all. "And that's common."

"Yeah, they used to have one module they put us through," the police officer who'd spoken up a minute ago, Manny, said. "They're getting better with it now, more awareness campaigns, but it's not universal."

"This type of training in recognizing signs of trauma in yourself and others is still pretty uncommon," Jonathan agreed. "A lot of high-stress jobs—police, medical, fire, aircraft operations, military—tend to provide one-time support after a major incident, but it's impossible to predict what incidents exactly will cause PTSD."

With that, he moved the conversation on to other subjects, but Dylan kept glancing over at Liam.

Even if he wasn't here for himself, he was genuinely interested and trying to learn. From his questions, it sounded like he wanted to be better educated to spot it in his coworkers. Dylan's heart softened again. Despite the playboy he came off as, and all his flirting, there were too many hints of sweetness and genuine caring under his façade for Dylan to believe that.

"That was interesting," Liam told Dylan when the therapy portion of the meeting wrapped up, leaving them to knit for as long as they wanted. Usually some people took off right away, and others stuck around for up to half an hour, finishing projects or catching up with each other.

This was the perfect chance to get to know Liam a little more. "It was," Dylan agreed. "Think you'll come back next week?"

"Yeah. With the way my shifts work, I'll miss the next couple weeks, but then I'll be able to come to a few weeks."

"Shift work's brutal," Dylan frowned in sympathy. The shifts here weren't too bad, as it was a pretty small retail store. Overnight shifts like firefighters did? That sounded a lot rougher.

"So is doing three part-time jobs at once, if you count being a student as a job, which you should," Liam pointed out, smiling at him. "How's this looking?"

"Yeah," Dylan chuckled. He reached out to take the square of fabric from Liam, holding his thumb over the tip of the needle to make sure no stitches slipped off. "That's good." It wasn't the *worst* job he'd seen.

"Liar," Liam teased, his eyes lighting up with amusement.

Dylan was startled into a laugh. "No, it's better than when I started!"

"Really?"

"I had fuckin' holes all the way down mine. I let a stitch slip. It was the worst dishcloth ever," Dylan lamented, and Liam's warm laugh made him smile.

"Well, I'm sorry, but I feel better, then," Liam teased.

Dylan laughed. "I'm glad. No, for a beginner, that's good work. Next time I'll get you to make a real dishcloth, with purling around the edges."

"Pearling?"

"With a U. It's like knitting, but backward." He could see Liam trying to work it out in his head and laughed. "Don't bother. I'll show you. Here."

He finished his row and transferred the needle with the stitches to his other hand, then looked up at Liam. "This is how you knit..." He didn't follow through, but he poked his needle through the loop to show Liam how it would go. "This is purling." After he pulled the yarn aside and went in backwards, he slipped the stitch to the other needle.

"Oh. That literally is... backwards." Liam looked intrigued. "This is a lot harder than it looks."

Dylan laughed. "Yeah, it is."

Liam picked up his knitting and Dylan put down his. "So you put the yarn here..."

Dylan's hands brushed Liam's as he reached out to hold the yarn back. "This way." Suddenly, Dylan became very aware that he was sitting close to Liam, their chairs almost touching. He could smell Liam's cologne. He could feel himself blushing, but he couldn't stop it. Thinking of ice didn't help a damn bit.

Liam's eyes flickered up to his, but he wasn't moving backward. He carefully looped the yarn around the needle, clumsily slipping his first purled stitch to the other needle. "Like this?" he asked, his voice low.

Dylan nodded. "One more," he encouraged him.

"From this to—oops."

Dylan's hand closed around the needle, gripping the tip just above where Liam slid his hand down to make room for his. The edge of his hand touched the tips of Liam's fingers, and his shoulder pressed into Liam's as he leaned in. His hands almost shook, his breathing quick as he picked up the dropped stitch and slid it back onto the needle.

He was warm all over, and he could hardly think straight. "There," he managed.

"Thanks," Liam murmured, finally setting the needles down and pushing his chair back. The move gave them a little more personal space. They were still sitting too close, but not practically in one another's laps now.

Dylan took the chance to take a deep breath, glancing around the rest of the room. Only a few people remained, and Jonathan was busy talking to them.

"You're very dexterous."

"Lots of practice."

"I bet." Liam's tongue flicked along his lower lip, and Dylan desperately wanted to taste those full, pink lips.

Liam was fucking hot, and he was right there—not recoiling when Dylan tucked himself into his personal space, but seemingly steadily waiting for Dylan to make a move.

Dylan wished he were brave enough. "Next week—er, next time—you'll make a proper dishcloth."

"I look forward to it," Liam smiled, rising slowly to his feet. "For now, I should get to bed. My days on start tomorrow."

Dylan felt disappointed that Liam was leaving already, but he reminded himself that Liam's job came first. "Yeah, of course. And I've got the clinic tomorrow."

"Good luck with that," Liam smiled, rising to his feet.

Dylan wasn't sure what to do, but he tentatively opened his arms.

Liam leaned in to hug him, those strong arms wrapping around his waist and shoulders as one broad hand rubbed between his shoulder blades. "Thanks for inviting me here."

"Thanks for coming out," Dylan murmured, desperately

trying to ignore the throbbing heat coursing through his body at the too-light contact between their chests, their hips carefully angled away from one another's. "Text me and let me know how work's going."

"I will."

I'll call... I'll be right back... see you soon. Unlike every other promise a big, muscled guy had made him and swiftly broken, Dylan believed this one.

The more he got to know Liam, the more Dylan believed he was a man of his word. Dylan wanted to tread carefully, because this guy wasn't just a hookup. He was fucking boyfriend material.

If that was what he wanted.

But Liam hadn't invited him upstairs again since that second meeting in the craft store. Instead, Liam seemed happy to be in his company, or to chat to him via text. Like he wanted to slow down, too, and see what happened.

Dylan didn't realize he was watching after Liam until Liam turned near the door, his eyes crinkling in soft amusement, and waved good night. Dylan hastily raised his hand in return, his cheeks flushing with heat again as he turned to gather up knitting needles.

7

LIAM

"You sure you're not gonna drag the curve down?"

"Hilarious," Liam rolled his eyes. He pretended to throw a handful of chips at Chris, across the living room of the fire-house, then crammed them in his mouth and dusted his hands off. He was at the table with his textbook open, scratching at his scalp with the end of his pen.

His fire science course was nearly over, and he really didn't want to repeat it this summer. His grades throughout the term had been fine, but the final exam was coming up this weekend.

Part of him wondered how Dylan studied, but that thought was stupid. He didn't need an excuse to invite Dylan over here. Especially not while they were still so uncertain of what they were. The other guys at the station knew; he didn't need to rub it in their faces.

"You're not gonna miss the class trip on Friday, then. I get to skip that," Chris bragged. "My exams are all morning."

"Lucky you," Liam mumbled, reading and rereading the section on fresh woods and idly hoping it would sink in deeper that way. In reality, he didn't mind being posted at the fire station that hosted grade-school field trip presentations on fire safety. They even had a mini replica of a house that they used to show how fire spread and get kids to demonstrate their newly acquired fire knowledge.

Kids were kind of cute. As long as he could count their grade number on one hand. After that point, all bets were off. Teens were a whole different ball game. But Liam had established his reputation as the guy who didn't mind them, which meant he was in charge of leading all the presentations now.

He wouldn't mind kids of his own someday. What about Dylan? Was he the fatherly type?

Whoa, that was wildly off-track. He was supposed to be studying, not mooning over the guy.

His phone went off and he put down his pen.

We got these hideous animal print fabrics in. V says they're hot.

Dylan had attached a photo of a stack of fabrics unfolded and overlaid so he could see a strip of each, and Liam sucked in his breath to keep from laughing out loud.

Yeah, he agreed with Dylan there. Cheetah, zebra, and a few other animals he couldn't name off the top of his head. They weren't even subtly patterned—they were obnoxious.

"What's so funny, dude?"

"Memes," Liam answered absently, not paying much attention to Chris as he texted back.

I'm dying here. Don't tell V but I hate them too.

Dylan was fun to talk to over texts. He chatted about what he was doing, or he sent texts like this one. He was way more interesting than most guys, who either sent dick pics after three texts or went silent.

And Dylan had used a lot of enthusiastic exclamation points after Liam had sent a photo of the engines being washed in the driveway that morning.

Liam still remembered that moment of Dylan crowding up into his personal space at the therapy group, his hands brushing over Liam's to guide him and take control for the delicate task of stitch recovery.

Every time they touched, his body jolted with interest. His cock really wanted to get to know Dylan's in those moments, as much as his brain told him to slow down and get to know him personally, too.

As if on cue, Dylan texted back.

It's slow & boring here.

Here too, Liam answered.

What's good for the gander is bad for the goose :(

It took Liam a second to get that one, but then he had to stop himself from chuckling again.

Would it brighten up your day if I dropped by?

To be fair, his mission wasn't just to see Dylan. He also had to grab groceries for the kitchen here, and there was a store just down the road from the Green Door and his apartment. That was the only place in town that stocked the pasta sauce he really liked.

Yeah! Only if you can, though!

It didn't take him long to convince Chris to let him go on a shopping trip. He promised to bring back the two-bite brownies that Chris was hooked on, and Chris practically shoved him out the door.

The chimes on the eponymous green craft store door tinkled softly rather than obnoxiously rattling when Liam pushed the door open. It felt weird to be here, right under his own home, when it was work hours—like playing hooky—but he had an excuse.

"Oh, hey." Dylan was smiling broadly as he came toward the door, bouncing on his toes. "I didn't think you were serious." His eyes fell to Liam's uniform, taking in the logo and the details.

"Of course I was," Liam grinned, letting him get a good look as he tucked his thumbs in his back pockets. "I actually came to pick up stickers for my kids."

The look on Dylan's face told him what he'd said wrong. He looked stunned—not horrified or suddenly disinterested, interestingly, but just surprised. "Your... right, your kids."

"For the station! Tours!" Liam's cheeks were hot now. He was used to all the guys teasing him, calling them his kids. He hadn't thought about that before saying it.

Dylan burst out laughing. "Oh! Right. I was gonna say."

"No kids that I know of," Liam grinned, laughing along with Dylan as he led him down the paper craft aisle. "I'm pretty sure I'd know."

"Me neither," Dylan winked. "I'll keep you informed, though. You do tours?"

"Field trips."

"Right," Dylan chuckled. "I went on one when I was a kid." Then something closed off in his expression—abruptly, almost too fast to catch—before Dylan forced a quick smile. "Fourth grade. It was fun."

Liam's chest tightened. Again with the look on Dylan's face. He'd never asked why Dylan was at the knitting circle, but he wondered if it was more than work experience. "Right," Liam agreed. "All the schools here do it. It's at my station these days, so I'm in charge of them."

"How cute. You, covered in ten-year-olds." Dylan smirked. "That's why you were so good with them."

Though Liam groaned and roll his head back in mock

horror, he was smiling, too. "Yeah, once you know how to handle 'em, they're all right."

Dylan clicked his tongue and tossed his head as he stopped in front of a sticker rack, picking through some options before Liam could even take in the inventory. "I'd sooner take a dozen fierce old ladies who are angry that we can't match their dye lots." As usual when he joked, he deadpanned.

It made Liam grin every time. "Yeah? You can keep your old ladies who don't want you to leave until you've carried boxes into the attic for them and rearranged their furniture."

It was Dylan's turn to laugh as he handed over a few packs of stickers. "Can't say I've experienced that. People usually try to take boxes away from me, not make me lift them."

Liam snorted with amusement. Dylan's t-shirt hugged his slender body, and though he had the ripple of biceps that every guy did, he clearly didn't do anything to maintain them. It didn't make Liam feel any less attracted to him, though.

"Will any of these do?" Dylan asked, his light voice breaking Liam's momentary focus on his body.

"Uh..." Liam raised his brows. One was specifically fire-related, and there were a few other sets with Dalmatians and water. "Yeah, all of them work. Clever. I wouldn't have thought of dog stickers."

"You don't have a Dalmatian at the station, do you?" Dylan asked, wide-eyed.

Liam laughed. "Nah. I'd like one, though. You never know. I'll take twenty packs, then." He started to wander toward the counter. Much as he wanted to stay and flirt with Dylan all day, duty called, and he didn't want Chris and the guys left in the lurch if a call came in.

Dylan counted out twenty and stayed at his elbow to accompany him to the counter, where Velma stood.

"Oh, it's our favorite fireman," she said as she smiled

warmly at him. Since he'd moved in, she'd made a point of checking in on him now and then to make sure he was doing all right. As far as landlords went, he really couldn't complain.

He beamed back. "And my favorite landlord, of the one landlord I have."

"Someone's got an attitude today," she laughed, clicking her tongue in disapproval. "I'm sure if you had another landlord, I'd still be your favorite, right?"

"Absolutely, ma'am." He paid up for the stickers, very aware of Dylan still lingering by the counter.

As she tucked the receipt and stickers into the bag, she glanced between them. "Oh, for God's sake. It's like watching tomcats prowl around. Dylan, walk the nice man to the door, and one of you ask the other one out."

Dylan's cheeks went bright red as he stammered a syllable or two, then shut his mouth again and walked toward the shop door.

When the surprise subsided, Liam stared at Velma for a second. "How...?"

"What? You're not subtle," she informed him, then flapped a hand to indicate that he should follow Dylan.

"I... Right. See you later, Velma," Liam politely bade her goodbye anyway, trying not to rush for the door. There was something very embarrassing about their whole song-and-dance being put under the spotlight by a sharp-eyed old lady.

Still, with the way she'd smiled as she said it, it was sweet.

And she was right—they *were* prowling around each other, neither quite sure how to talk to the other about it.

Emboldened but still blushing, Dylan met him at the door, twisting his hands together behind his back as he shifted from foot to foot. "So, are you gonna ask me out, or do I have to do it?"

"Coffee?" Liam asked, to see what kind of date he had in mind.

"I'd love to. Good way to get to know each other," Dylan answered softly, which made Liam smile. The anxious knot unfurled in his chest and stomach. Dylan wanted to get to know him better, too. The point was underscored when Dylan reached out to brush his arm lightly. "Thanks for coming in."

"You're welcome." Liam's eyes fell to Dylan's lips for a second. He wanted to go for a kiss, but he wasn't sure the moment was right. Besides, better not to give it all away yet. Keep Dylan interested.

"After your shifts are done, let me know and I'll try to be free," Dylan smiled. "There's a cute coffee shop round the corner."

"Saturday? The one by the orange tree? I like that one," Liam answered. Sometimes on his days off, he went there just to be around people without having to talk to them.

Dylan's smile made his eyes crinkle adorably. "Great. Good luck at work. I hope it stays quiet."

"Thanks," Liam murmured, his smile fading slightly. That brought his attention back to his job. Chief Williams wouldn't like him standing around flirting instead of grabbing groceries and heading back to the station.

And he *liked* his job here. He was willing to go to some therapy circle he didn't even need to keep it. He didn't want to transfer again, like he had from Boston the *last* time he ran away from his problems. Getting trained and licensed again in a new state had been a huge pain in the ass.

Besides, this was the longest he'd talked to a guy without getting in his pants. If this was a mission to get him to stop hooking up with every guy who looked at him twice, it might just be working.

8

DYLAN

Saturday couldn't come fast enough for Dylan. Even work at the clinic dragged on, but he was too restless to do anything useful like fill out his last university transfer papers.

It was hard to say why this date was making him so nervous, except for the simple fact that he hadn't gone on a coffee date in *months*. Mostly, guys who wanted him tended to invite him straight to their apartments, and not much romance followed.

But Liam, despite the chemistry between them, was trying, and that meant so much to Dylan. God, Dylan felt the same pull toward the hunky firefighter. He just wanted to grab him and shove him up against the nearest solid object, but he reminded himself that he couldn't let Liam's muscles blind him.

He was going to make Liam do this the right way.

Liam crossed the street, jaywalking with a quick glance each way, and Dylan grinned as Liam reached his side of the road. "Hey," Dylan raised his hand and called out. "Rule-breaker."

Liam looked up and grinned, that chiseled jaw jutting forward as he up-nodded at Dylan. "Don't tell anyone."

"Your secret's safe with me," Dylan winked. He'd dressed in a cute, short-sleeved collared shirt with a subtle floral pattern. It looked like Liam had dressed up, too; rather than his usual jeans and fire station t-shirt, he'd gone with dark jeans and a polo shirt.

God, he looked so preppy. It was sweet.

"Phew," Liam winked. He stepped around Dylan to push open the door to the cafe and hold it for him. "Shall we?"

Dylan had to brush past Liam to walk inside, and a shiver rippled its way down his spine at the brush of heat when his shoulder touched Liam's.

Liam's broad hand settled on his lower back, steering him over to the counter. It was a subtle move, yet incredibly hot.

Dylan licked his lips as he glanced up at Liam, trying to keep his brain focused on coffee as they stood in line. "What are you getting?"

"Hopefully a latte. Nothing fancy," Liam shrugged. "And a breakfast sandwich."

Dylan was about to tease him about it being noon when he remembered Liam's schedule. "Slept in?"

"I got off work early this morning, wrote an exam at the university, and napped until now," Liam nodded. His arm was so close to being around Dylan, and Dylan imagined being pulled in and held against him. God, he was only a couple of inches shorter than Liam, but Liam's body made him weak in the knees. He'd gotten a good look at those biceps when Liam wore his t-shirts.

They probably weren't even intended to be tight t-shirts. He just filled them out properly.

"Nice," Dylan weakly managed. *Oh my God, pay attention.*

You can't even see his biceps right now. Stop that. "Sorry. I mean, not nice, but..."

Liam laughed softly and dropped his hand, reaching in his pocket for his wallet as they approached the counter. "What about you?"

"T-shirts always look baggy—oh. Wait. I mean. Shit. Breakfast. Sure, a breakfast sandwich and latte..." Dylan's cheeks flushed with humiliation as he ducked his head. He wished he could rewind these last few seconds, or reload a save file as if it were a video game.

Liam's eyes glinted with amusement. "Should I have gone for my station t-shirt? I was considering that."

"Shit, I'm sorry," Dylan laughed, covering his face. He couldn't look at Liam now, especially when he was getting that teasing look from him. "You must think I'm totally air-headed."

"No. I can take a compliment," Liam winked. He nudged Dylan. "Your turn to order."

"Oh! Sorry." Dylan wheeled about to face the counter, still positive his face had to be bright red right now. The cashier was smiling, which only confirmed his suspicion and made it worse. "Uh, I'll—a breakfast sandwich, option four, and an iced soy hazelnut latte, please."

"And I'll take a latte and breakfast sandwich two, please." Liam stepped up behind him with cash in hand. This was that awkward moment, but Liam glossed it over by glancing at Dylan and smiling. "It's on me. You sent me to a great therapist, my chief told me. I owe you one."

"Oh. Oh, cool." Dylan glowed with pride. He'd been lucky to get the co-op placement with Gary. "Thanks."

"No, thank you."

They grabbed their drinks and plates of food, then headed outside to find a seat under an umbrella for shade. The shop's little patio faced the quieter side street rather than the main road, State Street. It made for a nice nook where they could look down the street and enjoy the gorgeous little gardens and tropical trees the city maintained so well, but the crowds of tourists weren't passing them up close.

"Have you lived here all your life?" Dylan asked as they settled down at the table. He examined his sandwich—spinach, tomato, and egg. Healthy.

Liam's focus shifted from the street to Dylan, and he pulled his chair in. "No. Only a few years. I transferred here from Boston. Lived there since I was a kid."

"Oh, that's a big move." Santa Barbara seemed like the ideal place to move, so Dylan hardly had to ask, but he did anyway. "Why?"

Liam hesitated and took a few bites of his breakfast sandwich as Dylan did, too. There was a wrinkle in his brow. He seemed to be thinking through how to answer. That normally wasn't a question people hesitated about. *For the weather, great surf,* or *for school,* for example.

Dylan's interest grew as Liam swallowed his sandwich with a sip of coffee, then wiped his fingers.

"I got into a little trouble at work," Liam admitted. "Nothing bad. I was just... distracted. Bad breakup. I didn't want to stick around, so I asked for a transfer."

Dylan nodded slowly. *Starting a new life here. Not unlike everyone else, then.*

"Now and then, I've thought I should talk to someone about it, but... I just haven't dated since then."

"Oh. In... a couple years?" Dylan's eyebrows rose. A hot, smart, funny, playful guy like Liam? He was the whole package.

Then again, Dylan hadn't dated anyone in ages—his brief romance with a classmate had ended when the guy turned out to party all night and not have time for him. Before that was

Kai. He just hadn't met anyone since. Sometimes life didn't hand you a boyfriend on a platter.

"Yeah. I just sound like a loser now," Liam laughed and shook his head, polishing off his breakfast sandwich in a few more bites.

"No, no," Dylan rushed to reassure him. "God, no. I haven't dated in, like, a year and a half. And that only lasted like a month."

Liam nodded. "Not the settling type?"

Though his tone was neutral, Dylan almost bristled at the implications. "No. I won't settle for a bad relationship. I'm not desperate."

"I meant settling down." Liam looked taken aback, but he smiled. "But that's wise. I should have done that back in Boston."

Dylan blushed. "Oh. Yeah. Sorry."

Liam laughed gently and shook his head, wrapping his hands around his coffee cup. His eyes never left Dylan's, like he found him... fascinating. Not just hot. "It's okay. I should have clarified." He paused and sighed. "I guess I'm easy."

"You don't say," Dylan teased, winking to make it clear he was teasing while he stirred the ice in his drink with his straw.

Liam laughed, those brilliant white teeth flashing. God, he had a perfect smile. He must have had to go through braces as a kid. "I did come on kind of hard, didn't I?"

"I'm not complaining," Dylan assured Liam with a grin in return, drinking through the straw and trying not to make it totally suggestive. "But I like dates, too."

"Yeah. Me too." Liam sounded sincere about that. "So, uh, I didn't ask. Did you grow up here?"

"Born and raised. Well, dragged up," Dylan joked.

Liam laughed and raised his brows. "Oh?"

"My mom's kind of a hippie. Just about off-grid, out in the

foothills." Dylan rolled his eyes. "I was homeschooled from sixth grade on."

"Oh? How did you like that?" Liam asked.

Dylan chewed his lip for a second. He didn't want to tell Liam the whole story yet. *I got beaten up and I still panic around crowds* tended to inspire pity and horror, not warm and fuzzy first-date feelings.

Instead, he smiled. "It was good. I learned a lot more. My mom was an all right teacher, but I studied myself a lot. Started studying psychology in high school, so by the time I got to college, I was more than ready."

"That's great," Liam nodded. "I'm finishing up a fire science course, actually. Working through a degree, slowly."

Dylan blinked. "Oh! Really? What does that involve?"

"Uh... a lot of what's on the tin," Liam laughed. "Just science and fire. No, really. I'm not being a smartass."

Dylan eyed him skeptically, then gestured with his drink at him. "I think you might be."

"All right," Liam relented and grinned. "We study things like... how fire spreads in forests, the melting points of different materials..."

"Ohhh." Dylan nodded. "So less Mythbusters, more..."

"Science." Liam laughed, leaning back with his cup. It was warm outside already, but he didn't seem to mind the heat against his hands.

"Do you have a high heat tolerance from the job?"

"I... What?" Liam took a second to understand what he meant, then looked down at the cup and back up at Dylan. His expression was surprised but thoughtful. "I... never thought of that, but maybe. I don't mind coffee on hot days, anyway. I wouldn't go make a four-course hot meal."

Dylan grinned. "Yeah. You must be almost used to the heat here now anyway."

"It still surprises me sometimes in the summer," Liam admitted. "But it's beautiful here. I love it. I don't regret moving for a second."

"Is your family back in Boston?"

Liam nodded. "I see them once a year or so when I take off for vacation, but that's about it. We aren't really close, though."

"Yeah. I know the feeling," Dylan murmured, then nearly dug his nails into his cup. Stupid comment on a first date. Nobody needed to know how weirdly distant his mother was. That was, like, textbook crazy.

Liam wasn't looking freaked-out, though. His expression was gentle as he watched Dylan. "So, you're interested in art therapy because you had shitty therapists and you want to do better?"

"Pretty much," Dylan smiled. That was somewhat a change of topic, at least. "Gary's great. I've sat in on a couple sessions and I learned a lot. I want to intern or do a co-op or something for an art therapy clinic specifically next, but we'll see. It gets competitive."

"Right," Liam agreed. "Gary did seem great. I'm looking forward to talking to him, even if... I don't know, I don't think I need to," he chuckled.

"Mmm," Dylan nodded slightly. "Your chief was just worried about the stress?"

"That, and..." Liam was blushing, his cheeks going ruddy red. "Uh, I did something dumb. Totally not first-date material."

Dylan snorted with amusement. "We're blowing right past first-date material already. Go for it. I won't judge you —probably."

Liam cracked another grin. "Probably. Okay. I missed the start of my shift."

"Okay?" Dylan could see how missing work would be worse for a firefighter than a craft store employee, but therapy?

"Just totally forgot. Because I was with a guy. Nobody important, either. Just someone who wanted to hook up with me, and I said yes."

Dylan nodded slowly. He knew the type: there were hookups that he wanted, and those he just said yes to. "And your chief thought that was a problem? The gay thing, or...?"

"No, no. He's gay too."

"Really?" Dylan stared. "That's awesome."

Liam smiled back at him. "Yeah, I thought so too. He told me, off the record, that he's worried. Probably because I can't seem to keep a guy around. So I guess I should warn you, too."

Warning? Hell, no. Dylan was only more interested. "That you don't tend to stick around, or they don't?"

"Ouch. The hard questions already." Liam put down his coffee cup and leaned forward. "I guess, if you're asking, both."

Dylan nodded. "Me neither, but more them. I wouldn't mind dating. I just attract assholes who want a little twink for the night, but they don't wanna be seen with me..." he trailed off. Shit, that sounded self-pitying.

"Yeah," Liam murmured. He clearly couldn't understand, exactly, but he was empathizing. "Sorry. That's frustrating."

Dylan blew out a little breath. "Yeah. So, have you thought about therapy for that? Or is that what your chief was thinking?"

"Oh, God, I don't know." Liam blew out a little sigh. "He doesn't know about that, I don't talk about my love life a lot around the station. I'm not closeted, but I don't wanna push it, you know? But yeah, maybe I'll talk to Gary after all. I get forgetful is all. The whole missing-work thing can't happen."

Dylan nodded. "It could help. And you're already halfway

through the waiting list. If there's a cancellation when you're off, you want me to let you know?"

"I'm not tripping over myself to go," Liam admitted with a laugh, "but yeah. At least to keep my chief happy. Don't think he was sold on the group therapy. He sort of eyed me and then said *all right*." He let out his breath and sipped his coffee again. "Well, that was kind of deep. How about a better topic?"

Dylan laughed. "Yeah. Tell me more about your job."

"You just want to picture me in my turnout gear," Liam winked, and Dylan blushed again as easily as that.

"I'll admit nothing." Dylan winked, then leaned in to listen to Liam talk about his daily routine at the fire station.

Not only is he a total sweetheart, he's a hero... but not one of the guys who thinks of himself that way.

Sure, he could pick out several symptoms of PTSD already in the guy, but given his job, that was no surprise. Maybe he liked to numb himself with sex, but Dylan was forewarned. Right now he was being honest and open.

Not just because of his job, Dylan trusted Liam already. He just hoped he was right, and Liam wasn't the kind of guy to break his heart.

9

LIAM

They'd been talking for almost an hour, and Liam was on his second coffee. He couldn't remember the last time he'd had this much fun just sitting down and talking to someone. Sure, he still wanted to kiss Dylan until his knees went weak, but he was able to shelve those thoughts for a little while to enjoy the moment.

For that matter, he couldn't remember the last time he was so stuck on wanting a guy. Usually he just shrugged and moved on when someone didn't want to come home with him as soon as he asked.

But Dylan? Holy fuck, he *liked* Dylan.

There was obviously more Dylan wasn't quite letting on, but that was fair enough; Liam had his own shit he didn't talk about, even on an unusually honest first date.

"It's kind of annoying being... you know, fem as hell," Dylan laughed quietly. He ran his pinky around the rim of his coffee cup, then stirred the ice.

Liam had been a tough kid for as long as he could remember. He hadn't been the kind of kid to pick on others, but he didn't understand what it was like, either. It was uncomfortable thinking about all the guys he took home who'd sneer at Dylan for being camp. "I bet."

"It's better here than probably anywhere else, I bet, but still," Dylan shook his head. "It was like homeschooling was a punishment for it."

They'd already touched on Liam's big flaw not even fifteen minutes into their date. This was getting close to something raw in Dylan—Liam could tell from the way he shifted in his seat. But it also sounded like something Dylan wanted or needed to talk about to someone. "You didn't like homeschooling all the time? Nobody likes school all the time anyway," he assured him.

"No, I know," Dylan chuckled. "I liked the education. But my mom would be happy never talking to anyone for the rest of her life. I like being social, around other people. Or... I did, anyway." He looked guilty now as he glanced down. "I suppose that's what I should warn you about."

Liam shook his head. He hadn't intended to warn Dylan about his own tendency to love 'em and leave 'em, but it had sort of slipped out. "We're not filling out disclosure paperwork here," he laughed gently. "You don't have to talk about anything."

Dylan looked grateful, but he shook his head. "No, I don't mind. People usually just freak out and apologize about it and stuff. I find it hard to be around crowds now is all. I've been working on it."

"You've gone to college, yeah? That must've been hard," Liam said, propping his chin on his fist, his elbow on the table. That was something small but important: he wasn't worried about sitting up straight and letting Dylan look him up and down. By now, he was more interested in what Dylan had to say than in making himself look hot enough to keep Dylan interested.

It was his conversation and company Dylan seemed to enjoy most, even if he caught Dylan looking more often than his date wanted to admit.

"It was. God, yeah. I'm actually really... nervous about university," Dylan admitted with a quiet laugh. "UCSB."

"That's where I'm doing my fire science degree," Liam told him, smiling gently. "Started off at the community college. The environmental science school is doing a test program now, and we're the guinea pigs."

"Oh, cool! So you transferred too?" Dylan lit up. "Can you help me?"

God, yes. Liam couldn't say no to that face. "Of course. When's the deadline?"

"Soon," Dylan groaned. He fidgeted and played with a stray hair on his jaw. "I don't know exactly when."

"No problem," Liam told Dylan. He leaned over the table impulsively to press his hand over Dylan's fist until Dylan's hand relaxed. He kept his voice soft and low, like he were talking to a scared pet to coax it out of a burning building. "We'll sort it out."

Dylan drew a deep breath, then let it out, focusing on Liam's eyes. "Thanks. I just panic. I don't know the campus, or anyone there... it gets overwhelming."

"I know a bit of the campus, and there's maps for the rest," Liam smiled. If Dylan needed help figuring it out, he could do that.

Dylan looked sincerely grateful, and he reached out to run his hand up Liam's arm, leaning in over the table. "Thanks a lot. You don't have to."

"I want to," Liam told him firmly. This was something else he could do besides worry about his final grade and wait for the next course to begin, throw himself into work, and... yeah, blindly hook up.

Dylan was sweet and driven, and Liam really believed he could make a difference in his chosen field as soon as he graduated. He was so easy to talk to. Nobody else could have coaxed so many personal details out of him in the first twenty minutes and still made him feel all right about it.

And for damn sure, nobody would have gotten him to agree that maybe he needed therapy to talk through his old relationship and how he'd run here, and how he could avoid forgetting important things like work and his hookups' names.

His instinct the first time they'd met had been right. There was something special about Dylan, and Liam still wanted to know what it was.

1 0

DYLAN

It turned out Liam was right: the transfer was dead easy. He'd already been pre-approved for a Summer Start entrance to the university assuming his grades were adequate, so he had minimal paperwork to do before he was formally accepted. The thought of walking around campus in September when the real crowds came still made his appetite vanish, but he was positive the early start would help.

Learning about a therapy appointment cancellation normally made him groan. Working through the waiting list for people who'd answer the phone and who were free on that particular date and time could be time-consuming. Instead, the next cancellation they got thrilled him, because it was on Tuesday afternoon, for Friday.

Liam was off today, so he could answer the phone, and he was off on Friday.

Still, he had to go through the formalities. He dialed the three people ahead of him on the waiting list, and when none of them answered, he pumped his fist.

"Hey, Liam. This is Dylan from the Green Tree clinic."

"Hello, Dylan from the Green Tree clinic. What a name you have."

Dylan resisted the urge to giggle. He was at work; he had to pretend to be professional with their client. "Er, we have a cancellation that's just come available for Friday afternoon at two o'clock. Could you make that day and time?"

"Mmm." Liam hummed, and Dylan had the sense he was thinking more about whether he wanted to than whether he could.

"My shift's over after that appointment slot is done," Dylan tossed out there, crossing his fingers under the desk.

"Oh. Is it?" Liam's voice was warm and amused, and Dylan blushed. That was pretty forward of him, but Liam was no less flirtatious. "I'd be happy to take your open slot."

Oh, fuck. It wasn't the first time Dylan had thought about that innuendo, but hearing it from Liam's pretty lips? Even if he couldn't see them, he could imagine Liam's tongue darting across his full lower lip, his eyes on Dylan's lips like he wanted to claim them for his own...

"Right," Dylan said, a little too forcefully. "I'll schedule you for Friday at two."

"I look forward to it. Thanks for calling," Liam answered. "Talk to you soon."

With the waiting room empty and a moment of privacy, Dylan put his forehead down on the desk, trying to will away his blush. His phone went off a second later and he groaned, then sat up and checked it.

You sound cute in receptionist mode.

Dylan's cheeks were hot all over again. Fuck.

I bet you're hot in fireman mode.

A minute later, he had an answer.

You wanna see sometime? Or ride along? ;)

Dylan grinned and didn't hesitate to answer.

Fuck yeah!

They chatted a couple of times a day via texts now. Sometimes they shared what they were cooking, and other times they texted each other links to interesting articles online or told jokes. It was easy and fun to talk to Liam, even if they tended to slip into flirting within a few messages.

I'll have you over sometime then :) Gotta go, driving to a buddy's for a BBQ.

Despite himself, Dylan felt a pang of worry. He knew it was stupid to be jealous when they hadn't even kissed yet. He tried not to sound like a jealous lover as he texted back.

Have fun, haha. :)

Liam answered moments later.

Less fun than seeing you, but I'll make do. ;) TTYS.

Dylan chewed his nail as he put down his phone.

They'd hugged again, this time for a long time, at the end of their first date, but something was still holding them back. Velma had complained a lot about him being worse than a tomcat when he headed to the store for his Saturday afternoon shift after the coffee date. He was aching to at least make out with Liam for as long as he could without getting blue balls. If Liam was feeling the same, Dylan couldn't blame him for blowing off steam.

It sounded like this really was just a friend, but Dylan chewed his lip still as he put his phone aside. The more Liam talked about his style of relationship, the more Dylan suspected there was something else going on. It clearly wasn't a deal-breaker, but it did give him pause.

If his suspicion was right, seeing Gary was going to do wonders for Liam. What if it turned out Liam *didn't* have a problem, or if he refused to go? Dylan still wasn't going to jump in bed with the guy, but next date, he wanted Liam's smartass mouth on his own.

Jesus. He was stopping this train of thought now, before he wound up jerking off in the staff bathroom. Something about Liam—something more than his broad shoulders and roguish smile—got under Dylan's skin. And it wasn't a mystery he was about to solve. The more they talked, the more interesting Liam seemed.

Wait. Maybe he *could* solve that mystery.

Shit. I like him. A lot. And I've never even kissed him.

Dylan put his face back down on the desk and stayed like that until the front door chime jangled to announce their next patient.

11

LIAM

"Tell me more about that."

This first session was even more awkward than Liam had imagined. He'd been skeptical of how well a moving light could help him process traumatic memories when he didn't even think he had that much wrong with him. It all sounded a lot like a hoax to him, but everyone insisted that Gary was great.

And, to be fair, Gary had given him the no-bullshit summary—this therapy had been developed for vets and proven effective in scientific studies. Compared to that kind of stuff, there was nothing to worry about. No harm in Liam trying it.

He talked a little about what he thought the problem was, and then Gary got him to watch the light as it moved back and forth, running with whatever thoughts came to mind. When they stopped, Gary asked him what he was thinking about and if any new images or thoughts had come up.

Liam's thoughts laid a bizarre path to follow: he'd started talking about his frustration about the chief thinking something was wrong with him, then his annoyance at himself for zoning out and forgetting about work. He was proud that his job was the one thing he always did right. He told Gary that he was going on dates with Dylan, before he could stop himself; he was glad when Gary's reaction was just a knowing smile.

His thoughts had skipped past the shallowness of his hookups—what he'd thought was bothering him—and straight on to his last relationship.

"After we'd been together for a bit, I started getting really weird about sex. Whenever we planned it ahead of time, I just..." Liam trailed off, his chest knotting in frustration. "I didn't like it. That's why I go for spontaneous hookups now."

Where the fuck was that coming from?

"I see. Be curious and notice what comes up for you when you think about that."

Again, the LEDs on the stand set up beside Gary flashed back and forth, and Liam reluctantly followed the light with his eyes. He wanted to look down as he thought, but this forced him a little more out of his comfort zone.

When the lights stopped, his heart sank. His mind was on that random guy—the one whose name he couldn't even remember.

"Wanna feel them somewhere else?"

"Duh."

Yeah, he wanted the stranger's lips on his dick. Who wouldn't?

As the guy sank to his knees on the ground, the rough ripping sound of his zipper coming down filling his ears, his hands shook. Even his thighs trembled until he clenched them harder, standing tall.

He'd thought at the time it was lust. Now, as he peered at the memory, his gut was clenching with a new realization. Maybe it wasn't a good sign. Maybe, every time he'd felt a

guy in a club grab his dick or made eye contact with a hunk
across the street and started to shiver...

Maybe the adrenaline was something else.

And he had the horrible feeling he knew what it was.

"Liam?" Gary prompted gently.

"Um." Liam stalled for time, twisting his fingers together as he stared down at the carpet. Gary was waiting for him to answer.

"Where do you feel this memory in your body?"

Other than all over? Liam had to step back for a second to think about it. He felt it in the pit of his stomach, and in his hands. He pointed to his stomach, then drew a breath. His hands were shaking, just like they had when Harry—

Shit, that was his name. Harry.

When Harry had hit the ground, he'd made some comment about Liam being nervous. As always, Liam had brushed him off with a quick, "Nah. I do that when I'm really fuckin' horny."

And just as everyone did, Harry had accepted that.

"I... I might get panicky during sex. Especially when it's planned ahead of time, like my ex noticed." How hadn't he noticed that before? "But even hookups. Shit."

Gary's voice was calm and steady. "What images are coming to mind for you?"

"The hookup that got me in trouble, and..." Liam closed his eyes against the white-hot pricks of tears in the corners, but the one swimming to mind couldn't be blocked out that easily.

"Don't tell anyone. If you do, I'll... I'll smash this over your
head."

Aaron overshadowed Liam as he trapped him against the
back of the house. They were in the shade, away from the
window. Aaron was one of Liam's friends' older brothers, but

*he wasn't old enough to drink: sixteen or seventeen, maybe.
But Aaron was home alone, his parents off somewhere, his
little brother—Liam's friend—not home.*

It was just the two of them.

*Aaron had a beer bottle in one hand and his dick in the
other. Liam couldn't stop staring at the beer bottle. Cold
droplets ran down the outside, the label soggy. It was a shitty
beer—he knew that much. His dad hated beer like that.*

Liam drew a deep breath, his chest so tight he almost
couldn't breathe. He hated that his voice shook as he answered.
He wasn't the kind of guy to just get teary over stupid shit.

"It was nothing. I thought I was over it."

Gary was still patient with him—gentle, but firm. "Do you
want to tell me about it?"

"I... I guess I have to, to get any further." Liam was logical;
he knew that. They couldn't put out a fire without breaking
down the door and striding in.

But kicking in the door fed the fire with fresh new oxygen.

It was going to get worse before it got better.

Liam was surprised how lighthearted he felt considering everything that had happened in his hour with Gary. After telling
him about that stupid fucking afternoon, that hour that he'd
written off as some stupid childhood shit and decided not to let
hold him back, he'd cried.

He'd put himself back together again, slowly. The memory
hurt less when he and Gary were done. He stopped shaking,
and he started thinking straight again.

But something had shifted. It was like meeting a terrified
little kid inside himself. Every guy he'd taken home, every late-

night drunken hookup—he saw them all in a different light now.

What if he'd been mistaking panic for lust the whole time?

That explained why nobody else felt the need to get their clothes on and leave as fast as possible, and why he hated thinking about hookups the next day even more than most people did. It didn't explain why he couldn't seem to stop hitting on men, though. Surely even his fucked-up perception of panic and lust had to know it was bad to induce this kind of state.

Gary told him they'd talk about that next time, and he guided him through finding a happier place inside himself. It was just like in meditation, when he was back in his bunk at the fire station, calming down his adrenaline after a dangerous situation to try to catch some sleep.

He surprised even himself when he greeted Dylan with a broad smile as he and Gary emerged from the treatment room. "Hi."

"Hey," Dylan answered, his eyes lighting up as he glanced between them. "What can I do for you?"

"We'll need another appointment scheduled for next week, please," Gary told Dylan with a smile. "And then you can take off for the day. I'll lock up."

Dylan straightened up, glowing with pleasure. "Oh. Thank you. So, um, this time next Thursday? I think we have an open slot..."

"I'll take it," Liam nodded. "Thanks."

"Perfect." Dylan nodded at Liam. "It's booked." He shut down the computer with a quick glance between Gary and Liam.

Liam cast him an apologetic look, trying to mentally communicate that he'd told Gary about them.

Gary saved him the trouble. "Enjoy your date," he told them with a chuckle, shooing Dylan off.

Dylan's blush as he came around the desk was totally worth it, even if Liam felt a little sheepish. "Thanks, Gary. See you next week."

"See you. Bye, Liam."

"Thanks, sir," Liam answered Gary with a quick jerk of his chin as he headed for the door. "See you next week."

The fresh air did wonders for him. He didn't say much for a minute as he ambled toward his car, his mind on the session. Dylan had come to a halt outside the clinic.

"So, um... you feeling up for that date?"

"Oh, God, yes." Liam tried to bring his mind back to Dylan. "Sorry. It was just intense."

"No, it's fine. I totally understand," Dylan assured him. "If you don't wanna go out or whatever..."

"Come back to my place?"

Dylan smiled for a moment and tilted his head as if thinking about it, then nodded. "I'd like that." He nodded toward his own little blue car. "I'll follow you there."

"Great."

That gave Liam a few minutes in the car to properly shelve his feelings about that session until next week.

Something was already changing inside him; in inexplicable ways, he could physically feel it. His chest had warmed up, and the energy that felt stuck in his stomach when he thought about his own reactions to men had loosened a little.

And now he had the insight of clarity. As much of a shock to the system as it had been to reevaluate his entire adult dating life, everything felt like it was in focus now.

He wasn't wondering why he was so horny anymore. There was a word for that, one Gary had used: hypersexual. And one more: PTSD.

Fucking hell, Chief Williams had been right.

Unlike the first time he'd asked Dylan home, he was pretty sure he wasn't going to jump Dylan's bones. As much as his body tried to tell him he wanted it, he'd ruled that out. But that didn't mean he was a monk.

He could feel it in the way Dylan's eyes fell to his lips and they stood close for a second, both hesitant to go to their cars. His body tingled with pleasure at the brush of their hands as Dylan leaned in for a quick hug.

Maybe Dylan wanted to take it slow, but they both wanted to kiss by now. Dylan's quick, shy glance back at the front door of his clinic told Liam that the public eye was the only thing holding him back. By the end of this date, they were going to kiss.

1 2

DYLAN

"You have PTSD?"

Dylan kept his voice calm and not judgmental. It wasn't unexpected, and he knew how to react to disclosure. Liam's feelings had to be raw right now.

"Yeah. Who'd have thought, huh?" Liam frowned. "If that's a problem... you know, romantically..."

Dylan smiled, leaning across Liam's small bistro table where they both sat, each with a cup of tea. "Not at all," he said, touching Liam's hand. Their knees brushed, and neither of them had pulled back. It was intimate, but not necessarily sexual right now. Dylan sensed that Liam just wanted to talk, and he could be that listening ear. "I've got my own issues."

Liam's brow furrowed. "Yeah. Have you thought of... getting therapy, too?"

Ah, yes. The therapy effect: people who'd had a successful session were the biggest evangelists of it to everyone else. Dylan bit back his amusement and smiled lightly as he shook his head. "No, I don't want to."

"You don't? But you want to be a therapist?"

"I'll start getting sessions after I become one to deal with what I hear in it, yeah," Dylan told him. "But not on my own accord. I've had it before and it was fucking useless. I just get a little panicky in crowds, and I deal with that with knitting and avoiding crowds."

"Isn't avoidance..." Liam bit back the rest of his sentence and smiled apologetically, holding up his hands to show he was letting it go. His eyes were worried, though.

Dylan laughed under his breath. Now Liam was trying to diagnose him? He was too sweet. "I'm gonna be fine," he assured Liam. "I've been coping with this for a long time. Classes won't be fun, but I'll get there."

"Okay," Liam agreed.

Dylan's chest warmed, and he shot him a look of gratitude for taking him at his word. "I'm glad I met you."

Now Liam was smiling, shifting his legs a little so their knees bumped again. "Me, too." Liam paused for a second, making Dylan tilt his head curiously. Liam reached out to cover Dylan's hand with one of his own.

He still wants me.

"I don't know what this diagnosis means for me," Liam admitted, his voice clear and low as he met Dylan's eyes. "But I know I'm interested in you. How are you feeling?"

If this was time for honesty... "Other than desperately wanting you to kiss me?" Dylan grinned. He saw that flash of *wanting* in Liam's eyes, and it made him hungry. It was hard to focus on sweet conversation when his body ached to have Liam in his lap on the chair, Liam's arms around his shoulders as they lazily kissed...

"Well, that's a hot thought," Liam murmured, his thumb stroking Dylan's fingers. He didn't look away, but his tongue darted over his lower lip.

It occurred to Dylan that the PTSD Liam mentioned might

tie into what he'd said about hooking up with guys, in which case... Liam might not be ready for sex. "It's up to you, though," Dylan said. "We can be friends for now, or take it slow."

"Kissing's fine. I like taking this slow, though," Liam admitted. "Which is not something I thought I'd ever say. Normally one of us would be on our knees by now."

A startled laugh escaped Dylan. He liked Liam's boldness and honesty; he knew exactly what he meant. "Yeah." When he found a hot guy who wanted to look at him more than once, and who didn't seem afraid of him—either in private or public... most of all, who genuinely enjoyed talking to him... Well, he'd always thought that *if* he found a guy like that, he'd get him in bed as soon as possible.

Now, though, he was finding that resisting the temptation was half the fun.

"First, though," Liam murmured, shifting in his seat. "Can I kiss you?"

Dylan turned over his hand to run his fingers along Liam's wrist, then up his palm to the tips of his fingers. "Please do." He leaned in over the table, and then Liam's hand was cupping his cheek, and his warm lips were pressing against Dylan's... and...

Oh, *fuck*, Liam was a good kisser.

Dylan swallowed his moan as he parted his lips, his scalp tingling with the touch of Liam's fingers. Liam kissed slowly but sensually, his lips sucking Dylan's lower lip, then his upper one.

The moment Liam let him, Dylan tilted his head and pressed their mouths together harder, the tip of his tongue sliding between Liam's lips again to tease him.

Liam caught it and sucked, his eyes devilish, and Dylan's cock was all the way hard in fucking *seconds*.

Dylan couldn't control his moan now, and it was a damn

good thing there was a flimsy little table between them, because his thighs twitched with the desire to press close to Liam.

Liam was rising from his chair and Dylan followed suit instinctively, stepping close to the firefighter as Liam's strong hands closed around his shoulder and hip, pulling him in.

Their bodies slotted together perfectly, Dylan's hard cock throbbing with need at the way their chests pressed and their knees brushed, but their crotches weren't quite touching. Both of them were trying not to dry-hump the other, but holy shit, was Dylan finding it hard... and finding his dick hard.

He felt when the tremor began in Liam's body—the moment he stumbled forward and ground his cock into Liam's thigh.

Shit. Dylan pulled back to give Liam space and catch his breath, and because they'd been kissing for an indecent length of time if they weren't going to go any further with it.

Liam was gorgeous, his cheeks all flushed and eyes hazy, lips swollen and rosy.

"Holy fuck, you are *hot*," Dylan breathed out. He didn't want to point out Liam's involuntary shudder, especially since it was subsiding now.

Liam's laugh echoed around his little bachelor apartment's kitchen as he slowly let go of Dylan, but he kept one hand on Dylan's hip. He looked more relaxed and steady now. His lips curled up in a smile. "Now it just sounds like copying if I say that, too."

"It does, doesn't it?" Dylan grinned.

Liam smiled for a moment before the expression faded and he seriously met Dylan's eyes. "I'm sorry if I act weird at all throughout this. I'm really into you, and it's... unusual."

Dylan blinked a few times. "You usually sleep with guys you hate?"

That made Liam burst out laughing. He let go of Dylan

and stepped back to rub his face. "Nah. I just usually don't like them."

He likes me, too.

Dylan was positive that either he'd fallen back into grade school—only this time, an alternate reality grade school where boys kissed boys and ran away on the playground—or he'd met someone that was worth a little embarrassment. His cheeks had never felt hotter. "Cool. Me, too."

"All right," Liam smiled.

"Hey," Dylan spoke up after a moment, nudging Liam. "There's a craft circle on Friday evenings for students. A de-stressing thing. You're a student, I'm a student... and I think we both need to de-stress."

It would get them into a public environment to help Liam stay as calm and self-assured as he had been during that coffee date, and it would help rid Dylan of the temptation to climb that fireman's pole.

Liam seemed to be thinking similarly, because his expression brightened. "You think Vee could use the help?"

Hearing his nickname for Velma from Liam made Dylan smile even more. "Almost definitely."

"Okay, then. Let's head downstairs."

For the first time, Dylan got to take the little side door into the shop; also for the first time, they were holding hands as they walked in.

It was worth the later teasing he knew he'd earned from Velma as she grinned at them both.

"About time you two showed up... looking slightly less broody, too. Come on, put that romantic energy to work and help me cut paper shapes for people's wish boards. Not all hearts, either."

Dylan laughed as he dropped Liam's hand and grabbed a stack of papers. "No hearts at all."

"Maybe a few hearts," Liam teased as he rounded the table to sit at the other side and grabbed scissors.

Dylan didn't like that wicked grin on Velma as she looked between them. "I have a few suggestions for yours." She cut two rounded shapes in the paper, and when she straightened out the scissors, Dylan saw where this was going.

"Vee!" Dylan laughed, covering his face with his hands. "Oh, God."

"What?" She innocently turned the paper again to keep cutting a third ball—no, a cloud shape.

As Liam's laugh rolled through the shop, Dylan couldn't look up from his hands, but he grinned. It was impossible not to smile when he heard that beautiful man laughing.

How lucky was he?

13

DYLAN

He was going to become one of those people who had no life and stopped by their workplace on days off to see how things were going.

To be fair, Dylan had only happened to be running errands in the area. He had to pick up groceries, and on the way back, he planned to stop by the bank and drop off a check for his mom. She rarely bothered to do her own banking, so that was his job.

It wasn't until he got to the bank doors that Dylan remembered it was Sunday. He nearly thumped his forehead with his own palm as he pocketed his check. To save himself the embarrassment of turning straight around, he casually glanced through his phone.

The rise and fall of high-pitched voices nearby sent an instinctive thrum of adrenaline through his body. His veins themselves flooded with nervous tension as his hand closed tighter around his phone.

"And that's when she told me, like, to get out. Can you believe it? What a bitch."

The kid chattering couldn't have been older than fourteen. She was in a group of about eight kids—both boys and girls, it looked like. A pack of young teens was just as bad as pre-teens.

They were coming toward him. Dylan froze, staring hard at his phone as his feet rooted to the ground.

One of the kids scoffed. "That's so gay."

Dylan didn't like the phrase, but he'd never be able to get a word out. It was stupid. He could move, smile, ignore them and walk away, but no. His body was going cold.

"Hey, gay boy."

The kids had blocked off his exit. They'd circled around him like animals. They all laughed. They were blocking his way to the buses.

Dylan looked down, trying not to engage with them. His mother had told him not to give them anything to latch onto. Imagine himself in a circle of white light. Smile and turn the other cheek.

"I'm going to be late for my bus."

"Oh, no. Little gay boy's gonna be late for his bus."

The kids were only his age, but he was scrawny and he looked young. His hair was long and fell into his eyes, unlike the other kids'. He was eleven, but he looked eight. Mom didn't like taking him to the hairdresser and he hated how she cut it, though.

Dylan tried to sound confident. These kids were just bullies. They always had been, since first grade. They'd never done more than shove him around. Maybe push him into a locker now and then. Hit him a couple times. Nothing bad.

"Leave me alone."

"Yeah? You and whose army?"

The girls behind Cory were giggling, not stepping in and helping. He'd never flirted with them, never flattered them.

No. It was Cory he wanted in a way that made him hate himself. If his face weren't twisted into an ugly sneer, he'd be cute. All he knew was that he wasn't supposed to think that.

Dylan doubled over when a knee hit his stomach. He curled in on himself, trying to protect himself.

The next thing he remembered was a siren, a teacher by his shoulder, the principal standing behind her, and a man in a dark blue shirt asking him where he hurt. The man had a hat that read EMT.

Dylan's cheeks were wet, and he didn't know if it was with tears or blood, but they stung when he started crying again when the man repeated his question. He didn't know where to start except, "Everywhere," but he couldn't get the word out.

This had to be a bad dream.

He closed his eyes tightly, but it didn't go away.

Dylan was watching himself fidgeting with his phone—opening apps and closing them again with the home button. Why was he doing that? He was going to drain the battery.

"Don't say that," another kid frowned.

And then they were brushing around him almost like they didn't notice him, heading for the door to the McDonald's right next to the bank. "Yeah, yeah. I forgot."

They were gone, but he was still standing by the bank doors, his heart hammering. He had to move.

Deep breath in, deep breath out. He did it almost unconsciously as he watched himself. What were those thoughts running on a loop through his head?

Get out, get out, get out.

Before the kids came back out.

His limbs like molasses, Dylan pushed himself away from the bank door. He couldn't drive yet, but he could take a walk.

Fucking hell. I can't even be an adult for two days, can I?

One foot in front of the other. State Street was quiet this Sunday early afternoon, but it had grown busier even since he'd put his groceries in the car.

He was close to the shop. That was a safe bet. He knew for a fact there weren't any parties there.

As Dylan walked, the fog gradually lifted. He started to feel more aware of his body's movements, of one foot on the ground and then the other.

Dylan started counting sights, sounds, smells, tastes, and feelings, picking a sense and counting down from five.

By the time he reached feelings, the sun's warmth on his skin was obvious again, and he realized how damn hot he was. The cold sweat had evaporated, and his shivers were gone.

He ducked into the Green Door and let out a breath of relief at the familiar scent—wood, paper, glue, yarn, all the best things in life mingled.

And, very faintly, a certain spicy cologne.

What was Liam doing here?

14

LIAM

No matter what he did, Liam couldn't remember how to slip-slip-knit. Dylan had showed him after that one knitting group, but every time he looked up a video on it and tried to do it himself, something went wrong.

He considered chewing his knitting needle in frustration, but blew out a sigh and put down his work instead. The project he was working on was simple: a knitted heart, just big enough to be a washcloth but small enough to be a coaster or a little ornamental decoration.

It was a lazy Sunday for him—his apartment was clean and stocked with groceries, he'd called his parents, and he was bored. He'd headed downstairs for a chat with Vee, and on the way up, he'd bought a couple of balls of yarn and some needles.

Liam sighed and swallowed his pride, shoving his feet into flip-flops and grabbing his knitting to head down the narrow stairs and through the side door into the craft store.

Velma was behind the counter, chatting to an older lady who was on her way out. When she saw Liam, she grinned. "I thought you might be back."

Liam blushed and resisted the urge to shove the knitting behind his back like a kid with his hand in the cookie jar when the customer turned to look at him and smile before she headed out.

He didn't think less of himself for knitting. It didn't threaten him. Still, the thought that a coworker might somehow find him here—one of the guys from the station, or one of their wives or girlfriends? Last thing he needed was a cute new nickname from Chris.

"Sorry. I can't get the hang of SSKs."

"Let's see your pattern, then." Liam had copied it down from the computer. He dug it out of his pocket, his cheeks still hot, and set his knitting on the counter. He was in the middle of the row, so he had to be careful.

If Velma noticed what the pattern would create, mercifully, she didn't comment. She just nodded at the knitting. "Oh, don't put that down. Show me what you're doing."

It turned out it was a simple correction. He was doing it backward, knitting two together instead. Liam wasn't certain he understood it, but he did his best to memorize the hand movements she showed him.

Before he could gather up his knitting again, the door jangled.

Liam could instantly tell Dylan wasn't himself. He was pale, and the way he looked around was like he was orienting himself.

Was he on shift now? Liam looked quickly over at Velma, who shook her head. She jerked her head toward Dylan, clearly indicating that he should go talk to him.

Liam pushed the project aside and headed for the door. "Dylan?"

"What're you doing here?" Dylan answered, then looked

embarrassed and quickly raised his hands. "Not that you're not allowed."

Liam laughed gently as he approached Dylan, keeping his distance so he didn't crowd up to him. "Just came down for help with a project."

"Oh. Right."

"Are you working today?"

"No. No, just dropping in for... uh, a few things," Dylan answered absently. At last, he blinked and met Liam's gaze. That was better.

"Something wrong?" Liam asked, lowering his voice so it was just the two of them.

Dylan hesitated, then rubbed his face. "It's nothing. It's dumb. Um, what are you doing today?"

"Nothing. You? Wanna do something?" Liam asked. It wasn't hard to guess—Sunday shoppers could be crazy, especially tourists. Dylan probably just got stuck in a crowd and got spooked.

Dylan frowned. "I have to visit my mom. She wants me to install this auto-watering system."

"That's a better excuse than washing your hair," Liam smiled, and his smile grew into a grin when Dylan's eyes twinkled.

"It's—I swear, it's the truth," Dylan laughed. "I'm shitty at home DIY stuff. God help her plants."

Liam laughed, too. "You want help?"

"You wouldn't mind?" Dylan pouted. "I'm such a loser. I can't even figure out water pressure."

Liam chuckled, snaking an arm around Dylan's waist to hug him into his side for a moment. "Would you call me a loser for forgetting how to do the SSK thing?"

"Slip-Slip-Knit? Of course not," Dylan frowned.

"Then you're not. It's just my job. I don't mind helping, if you don't mind me meeting your mom..." Liam trailed off, leaving that one up to him.

This wasn't like a *formal* parent introduction, surely? They were still in romantic limbo, neither speaking up about the *boyfriend* label yet, but both clearly interested... especially after that conversation on Friday.

"I'd like that," Dylan murmured. "I said I'd head over after I drop off groceries."

"I can pick you up to go there in an hour or something," Liam offered. He had nowhere else to be, after all. "Just text me the address."

Dylan was relaxed now, his hand on Liam's back as Liam still held him in a half-hug. "That'd be awesome," he agreed softly. Whatever had spooked him seemed to be a memory now. "Okay. I better go drop off my groceries before the milk spoils, then."

"That's a good idea," Liam agreed, finally dropping his hand from Dylan's shoulder. When Dylan leaned in, he met him halfway and softly pressed his lips against Dylan's.

Once they pulled back from the kiss, Dylan was blushing. "Cool. See you." Dylan strode out of the store quickly.

Liam bit back his laugh and resisted the urge to point out that Dylan hadn't picked up whatever he'd said he was here for. He had the feeling that had just been an excuse, anyway.

"Well, aren't you two just smitten?" Velma was approaching, holding his knitting and wagging his needles at him as she grinned. She handed back the pattern first, then the bundle of yarn and needles. "I think I know what you're knitting." Her grin turned triumphant. "Is it for him?"

Liam cleared his throat, his cheeks burning. "Thanks for the help, Vee." He chuckled at himself as he fled for the stairs, but her laugh rang through the store behind him.

He was just working on practice pieces. Hearts were a convenient shape to practice adding and subtracting stitches— that was all.

15

DYLAN

Ugh, Dylan still couldn't believe Liam *had* to be there right when he was having one of his out-of-body spells. That was twice now in, what, three weeks?

Thank God he hadn't looked at him like some kind of loser, though. He'd just stepped close, letting his physicality ground Dylan. Again, he'd talked calmly, distracting Dylan like he knew exactly what to do. Dylan had snapped out of it gradually, finding himself in that roomy but firm embrace and realizing what Liam was doing.

Sometime during all of that, he'd agreed to a date at his mom's house.

"Pick up," Dylan mumbled under his breath, then sighed heavily when she didn't answer her phone. Typical.

After her voice message played, he left a message.

"Hey, Mom. It's me. I'm on my way over in a bit. One of my friends is gonna pick me up and bring me there. He's a firefighter so he knows more about water pressure and stuff. I tried to drop off your check but I forgot it's Sunday, I'll do that tomorrow. Okay, see you soon. Love you."

The whole time, he stretched his neck back, recoiling away from the phone. He knew the message was decent—he'd gotten okay at leaving them with his receptionist work, after all—but it always felt so awkward.

He hung up and breathed his relief, then turned to scan his apartment. Everything could use a good cleaning. He had twenty minutes.

"Get working," he told himself. It worked out perfectly, because throwing himself into hard manual labor was one of the few foolproof ways to well and truly ground himself after getting a fright in a crowd.

He barely noticed time passing as he put dishes into the dishwasher, tidied up the living room, made his bed, and swept the floor. He even had the counters wiped down and the bathroom tidy before he heard the apartment buzzer go off.

"Hello?" Dylan answered into the panel in his wall, holding down the button when he spoke. He grinned, waiting to hear Liam's sexy, low voice.

"This is the fire department," the speaker crackled. "I understand you need help with the water pressure in your hose?"

Dylan's cheeks burned, and he leaned on the button as he laughed, then pressed the entry button to unlock the door for him. He leaned on the wall and kept laughing for a few more seconds, covering his face with his hand.

Liam was ballsy. Dylan liked that about him, even if he was still blushing when he opened the door.

"Is this the place?" Liam grinned, swaggering into the doorway and resting his hand on his hip, straight out of a porno.

"Stop, I can't look at you," Dylan begged, flapping his hand at Liam. He bent over to pull his sandals on, strapping his feet in, kind of hoping Liam would take advantage of the view. As he straightened up, he caught Liam's eyes flickering to his face.

Liam winked. "Sorry. I'll be good."

"At least around my mom, please," Dylan laughed. "Or she might try to adopt you with some tribal incense ritual."

Liam stared at him for a second as if seeing if he was serious.

"No, really. She's into a lot of weird stuff," Dylan warned him. "I turned out surprisingly normal, all things considered." He checked his pockets for his phone, keys, wallet, and SPF-factor lip balm. Once he was sure he had everything, he gestured toward the hallway. "Shall we?"

"I'd be delighted if you'd accompany me," Liam flirted in return, offering his arm.

Oh, God. Dylan didn't know how to take it. He gingerly wrapped his hand around Liam's bicep, resisting the urge to squeeze. He couldn't even close his fingers around his arm! How sexy was that?

He followed Liam out to his car, admiring it. It was a lot newer than his own, and sleek and red. Not that he was shallow enough to care about his ride that much until he could afford a better one, but his little blue beater station wagon did *not* fit his aesthetic at all. This one suited Liam. Letting go of Liam's arm to climb into the car was surprisingly disappointing, though.

"I'm looking forward to a little outdoor work," Liam admitted. "I don't get to do much of it these days."

"Right. You don't have a balcony or anything upstairs, do you?" Dylan asked.

Liam shook his head as he pulled out of the guest parking lot. "No, sir. I do get exclusive use of one windowsill that I think I could squeeze a plant pot onto."

Dylan laughed. "Have you tried?"

"No. I can't get over my fear of it falling and killing someone." Liam grinned. His grip on the wheel was loose and confident, and Dylan resisted the urge to stare at his arms even more. Damn his tendency to wear t-shirts. He *knew* what effect they had on Dylan. Flirty bastard.

"Wise," Dylan grinned. "My mom lives up in the hills, up that way."

Liam followed his directions easily. To Dylan's surprise, as soon as he named the street, Liam nodded.

"Oh. Most people don't know where that is. Oh, right."

"Firefighter," Liam grinned. "I could moonlight as the best damn taxi driver."

Dylan laughed. "There's an idea. Or a pizza delivery driver."

"That too! Do you often order delivery pizza?" Liam's eyes were sparkling. "From boys in crop tops?"

"Oh my God," Dylan groaned as the memory of that hunk leaning in his doorway and giving him the once-over popped back into his head that easily. "I don't need any more temptation, thanks."

"I'm just asking," Liam winked.

The traffic lightened as they left the city, fleeing the suburbs for the semi-rural hills that Dylan's parents had escaped to.

"So, just your mom lives up here?" Liam asked.

"Yeah. My dad died a couple years back." Dylan's chest tightened as he glanced out the window.

"Sorry," Liam softly said.

"It's okay. Cancer. Stupid, huh?" It had been four years; Dylan didn't get emotional about it as much these days, but it still stung now and then.

"Cancer's really stupid." Liam squeezed Dylan's knee lightly, letting him have a moment of silence.

Dylan met Liam's quick glance with a little appreciative smile. He touched Liam's hand before Liam let go to grab the wheel again. "Yeah. What about you? Your parents are both in Boston? Together?"

"Yeah, still happily married and all that," Liam told him. "And two brothers. One married, one kind of off the beaten track, but finding his way back."

Dylan nodded back, fascinated by this. He didn't have any siblings, which he'd once resented. Now he was kind of glad. He didn't need any more weird, strained family relationships to worry about. "Cool. You're the wanderer."

Liam paused thoughtfully, then smiled. "I guess I am. They called it *running away from my problems*, but same difference, right?"

They shared a laugh.

"Up that hill."

"Jesus, you'd have to be the Hulk to bike up here."

"Yeah," Dylan laughed as they twisted up the hill and around the corner into his mom's driveway. The property itself was pretty flat once they got up the driveway, but it always surprised people how steep the slope up there was. "I only did it for a few summers as a kid. Got a car right at sixteen."

"Don't blame you." Liam shut off the car and glanced at the house, and Dylan followed his gaze, trying to see everything afresh like he did. It was a little white house with tacky yard ornaments, Feng Shui desert-friendly plants in the front, and a fenced-in backyard where most of the plants he'd had to yank out had come from.

"The watering system's for the backyard, huh? You have it here already?" Liam asked as he climbed out of the car, and Dylan followed suit.

God, it wasn't even lunchtime and it was warm already. "Yeah, in the shed."

"Hello, Dylan." His mother was at the door, shading her eyes as she squinted at Liam. "Hello," she added to him, then looked back at Dylan. "I didn't know you were having a friend over."

"I called, Mom," Dylan groaned and led Liam up the path to the front door. "This is Liam. He's a firefighter. He knows more about hoses and stuff."

"It's very kind of you to help," his mother thanked Liam.

"Don't mention it," he waved off the thanks. "Pleased to meet you, Ms..."

"Waters. But don't call me that, please. Lynn's fine. Lemonade?"

"Yes, please," Liam said at the same moment as Dylan, and they swapped smiles.

"Come on through, let's get started." Dylan didn't want to hang around here longer than he had to, necessarily. He led Liam through the house, waving off Liam's attempt to take off his shoes when he came in. "Mom's not big on house rules like no-shoes."

"Life's too short for those," she called from the kitchen.

Dylan smiled at Liam and rolled his eyes. He could have used a few more rules here and there, but that was one he actually agreed with. "See?"

"Okay," Liam laughed, tugging open the sliding door as they headed outside.

It didn't take long for Dylan to show Liam where the garden beds and the kit were, and then they had the pieces spread out on the picnic table.

"Here you are," his mother announced, setting down glasses of lemonade and cookies. That was about the one motherly thing she knew—snacks. Every time Dylan came over, she brought them out. "How was your week? Did you drop off the check?"

She took a seat nearby and picked up her book.

"Thanks. It's Sunday," Dylan groaned, shading his eyes as

he squinted at her, then sipped from his glass. If she wanted honesty... "So, no to the check. I froze up in a crowd. It sucked. I'll deposit it tomorrow."

"Oh, dear. You haven't been seeing anyone for that? Darrell says he has a good tincture for that..."

Dylan bit his lip, then shoved a cookie in his mouth. "Tried it before, Mom, remember? Didn't work."

"I don't think you stuck with it long enough." She was already looking at her book, speaking absently like she was focusing more on her reading.

At fifty bucks every two weeks, he was pretty sure two weeks was long enough to stick with it. "Right," Dylan mumbled, looking over at Liam. A quick *I'm sorry, can I do anything* would have been better than this discussion.

Liam took the cue. "We'd better get assembling before the heat really sets in."

Thank you, Dylan mouthed and rolled his eyes.

Liam just squeezed his shoulder on the way past, then started to show him how the pipes fit together. Some were designed to drip-feed, and others passed water to another section. There were T-joints and L-joints and all kinds of things he nodded and smiled when Liam explained.

Mostly, he was interested in the way Liam was sweating now so his t-shirt clung to his chest. Christ, he had pecs. And his back... Dylan loved a good back.

"And... the pressure is halved... you're not listening, are you?" Liam laughed as he wiggled a joint into a pipe, then held out a hand for the tool that tightened a band around the joint.

Dylan's cheeks flushed and he pushed his hair back, out of his eyes. "I am! Sorry. I just don't get it."

Liam hummed. He looked distracted as he tightened the clamp. When he handed back the tool, he held it for a second longer to catch Dylan's eyes before he let go. "You're a lot smarter than you pretend."

Dylan opened his mouth, then closed it again, his cheeks flushing with heat. His mother had long since disappeared inside, and it wasn't like the neighbors could hear.

He ducked his head and stared at the joints he still held. "A lot of guys get intimidated. If you're... a cute little twink, that's all they want from you."

It was kind of embarrassing to have it thrown in his face, but he resisted the urge to get defensive. Liam was right, and the way he'd said it wasn't accusatory. It was a simple observation with a caring, warm note to his voice.

Like he'd already guessed.

"I like you clever," Liam told him. He ran his hand down Dylan's wrist to his palm to open it up, picking out the joint he needed, then caught his eyes.

Dylan looked at him for a long second before his gaze fell to Liam's lips. They looked warm and dry, but still full and pink and tempting. When he leaned in, so did Liam. Dylan's lip balm helped smooth the way as he pressed their lips together for a long few moments.

Liam kissed him slowly and sweetly, their lips sliding together for a long few moments before he pulled back and pressed his lips together. "Vanilla...?"

"Yes, I wear lip balm," Dylan clicked his tongue. "Sometimes it's even tinted."

Liam laughed warmly and squeezed Dylan's shoulder before he turned to slide the elbow joint into both sections of pipe for what looked like the last connection in the system.

As they tested the water, Dylan still felt the memory of that affectionate touch just as much as Liam's lips on his own.

"And now... you set up the timer so you don't break any city ordinances," Liam teased. They stood back to admire their work for a second, and Dylan reached out to rest his hand in the middle of Liam's back. His own t-shirt was damp, too, from sweating under the direct sun.

"I will," Dylan promised. "Thanks a million for this."

Liam looked genuinely pleased as he smiled back at him. "It's no problem. That was kind of fun. Like mechanical sets. You know, K'Nex? Was that what they were called?"

Dylan laughed and shook his head. "You couldn't talk me into those things. I was much too busy with my art sets. And chemistry."

"Ahhh, see? Clever," Liam wagged his finger. "What did you blow up?"

Speaking of rules I could have used. Dylan's cheeks were hot as he avoided Liam's gaze. "Um, a beaker... and one of Mom's favorite dishes. I never told her about that. And I started one fire."

Despite his laughter, Liam tapped a finger to his lips. "I pledge my silence," he teased.

There was a tap on the window, and then his mom pushed it open. "Lunch is ready."

"Thank you, ma'am," Liam answered and looked at Dylan. "Are we sticking around that long?"

Dylan smiled and nodded. "Sure. We can grab some food before we go."

His mom was kind of embarrassing, but Liam seemed to take it in stride, just as he did everything else. Dylan had never been more grateful.

If he could deal with Dylan's crazy *and* his mom's crazy? He was a keeper.

16

LIAM

What do you mean, bring pie or look up?

Liam tried not to grin as he kicked back on the sofa in the firehouse living area. He'd been flirting with the idea of having Dylan drop by over the last day or so. It was Wednesday and they hadn't seen each other since he dropped Dylan back home after lunch with his mom. He was getting impatient to see him.

On the other hand, there was the very real risk Chris might drop water on him.

Just trust me and bring pie :)

Apple OK?

You know the way to my heart. xox

"You can tell me who it is any time."

Liam looked up from his phone, almost dropping it on his lap. Chris had come up behind him and was resting his hands on the back of the couch, trying to lean over his shoulder for a look.

"Fuck off," Liam laughed at him. He tried to grab Chris's hair and pull him over the back of the couch into a wrestling match, but Chris ducked away just in time.

"I'm just saying, who is it?" Chris raised his eyebrows expectantly, circling the couch to sit on the coffee table instead. "A guy, right? What's his name?"

Liam's cheeks flushed. At least Chris knew—so did Kevin, the other guy who shared their shift, who was right now on engine maintenance duty. Most of them knew. It was nice. He didn't have to play the pronoun game or have *that* discussion. "I... It's not official yet."

"Not Official Yet? Brutal, even as nicknames go," Chris clicked his tongue solemnly.

Liam groaned. Chris was so going to figure it out the second Dylan walked in, so there was no point in being coy. "Fine. Dylan. He's coming for lunch today. Don't scare him off."

"I'm not," Chris raised his hands, looking innocent.

"He's bringing pie. Don't drop anything. He'll get pissed off if you fuck up his hair."

Chris laughed and groaned. He'd only dropped water on a couple of guys' girlfriends before being scolded by one, but Liam still wouldn't put it past him to water-drop a guy. "Oh, man. I never knew what your type was."

Liam punched Chris's knee and checked for Dylan's response.

I have some good guesses by now ;) See you this afternoon.

He answered.

Can't wait. Text before you leave.

Of course.

Chris was tapping his foot.

"Huh? Sorry."

"Jesus, you're in deep. I asked, where did you meet him?"

"Oh. Uh. The store near where I live."

Chris furrowed his brows as if working through that. "The craft one?"

Liam's stomach churned nervously. He'd admit to liking arts and crafts if he was caught, but he wasn't going to just hand Chris ammunition. "Yeah. He works there. His boss is my landlord."

Chris accepted the explanation easily. "Last few shifts you've been, like, smirking at your phone all the time, not sneaking off to the bathroom to use whatever those apps are."

"Fuck off," Liam snorted. "You're just jealous 'cause straight people don't have those apps. You have, like, Tinder or whatever."

"Yeah, and they're shit," Chris informed him, pushing himself off the coffee table. "What kind of pie?"

"Huh? Oh. Apple."

"Good. Nothing gross like rhubarb-whatever." Chris headed to the kitchen to check the cupboards for lunch ingredients. It was his turn to cook.

Liam twisted on the couch to see him. "You'd seriously look a gift pie in the mouth?"

"I'd look a rhubarb anything in the mouth, and then spit it out and ask why it wasn't a real food instead."

Liam shook his head as he pocketed his phone. "You have no taste. Chief's coming by today, right?"

"Yep. Why? Worried he'll sweep your boyfriend off his feet?"

Liam groaned but didn't answer. If he insisted they weren't boyfriends, Chris would make doubly sure to call them that when Dylan came here.

Good. Chief Williams was still coming by. That was the other, sneakier reason he wanted Dylan to drop by for lunch today, of all days. He was sure Dylan wouldn't mind.

All things considered, Liam thought he was doing a damn good job pretending not to be nervous.

"Oh, dig in," Chris waved at Dylan. "Chief Williams is probably buried in paperwork."

I hope he doesn't mind pranks. Liam was about to find out, one way or the other.

Sure enough, a minute after they'd all started to eat, Chief Williams walked in. He was a tall man with the kind of presence that commanded attention and respect. "You started eating without me?" Their chief shook his head at Dylan. "I hope you're not gunning for a job here, son."

Dylan went red and put down his fork, glancing quickly at Liam, Chris, and Kevin. To his credit, he didn't blame any of the others, just straightened up and nodded. "Sorry, sir."

Chief Williams let him stew for a few seconds before he smiled and went to grab his plate. "Kidding."

As Dylan groaned, the other three guys broke into laughter.

"You didn't warn me about *that* one," Dylan accused Liam.

"I can't spoil all their fun." Liam grinned. "I only keep you dry. The rest's up to you."

Conversation quickly turned to stories from the workplace, and Dylan stayed quiet to listen to them all. Liam knew damn well that Chris was exaggerating some of them, but he let him get away with it. After all, one of them from a duplex fire last year involved Liam chopping through a wall, and the story was impressing the hell out of Dylan.

Liam slowly relaxed as all the guys chatted with Dylan, who was on his best, most charming behavior. He let them tease Dylan a little, but thankfully, even Chris held back from making awkward relationship jokes.

He'd known they wouldn't get much one-on-one time here, but it was still seeing Dylan, and in a different environment than he had before. Dylan was getting on just fine with his buddies, and it made Liam think about what it would be like to have Dylan by his side at their barbecues or their kids' parties.

Not his *own* kids, obviously, but Kevin's, or one of the other guys.

After lunch was over and they'd shared the apple pie, Kevin washed up and Chief Williams thanked Dylan for dropping by.

Dylan took his cue to head out while it was quiet. "No, thank you for having me," Dylan said, smiling particularly at Liam, then looking between them all. "I've never been to a firehouse. Except as a kid, for the mandatory field trip, you know."

"Next time I'll show you the scale model we've got these days," Liam promised with a grin, rising to his feet to see Dylan out. "It's pretty cool."

"Do I get to see you in turnout gear?" Dylan had picked up bits of the lingo already—impressive.

Chris snickered. "If you're very good, I'm sure we can arrange that."

Dylan blushed, and Liam smacked Chris's shoulder on the way past to the door. "Thanks," Dylan told Chris dryly. When they had a private moment in the foyer at last, Dylan smiled at him, relaxing again. "They're cool."

"Yeah. Thanks for putting up with them." Just to make sure, Liam looked up, and Dylan followed his glance.

Dylan laughed. "I'm gonna have to bring pie every time, aren't I?"

"'Fraid so," Liam grinned. "See you soon, huh?"

"Tomorrow? After... Afternoon? I'm off a bit later, but I'll drive over and see you?"

Liam appreciated that Dylan wasn't blurting out that he was going to therapy in front of everyone else. He nodded quickly. "Yeah. That sounds good."

He didn't dare lean in for a goodbye kiss, but he squeezed

Dylan's arm as he opened the door for him. "Thanks for coming by."

"See you soon," Dylan promised and warmly smiled back as he strode down the driveway to the guest parking spots where his little blue car was parked.

Resisting the urge to gaze after him like a lovesick puppy, Liam shut the door.

He almost made it back to the kitchen before Chris piped up, "Someone's got a *boyfriend*. Look at you. All grown up."

Chief Williams was reading the memo book on the table but smiling to himself, clearly listening.

"If you're jealous, I can see if he's got any buddies," Liam retorted, heading about cleaning the living room before he headed out to the engine room to make sure everything was in order there and clean out the cabs of the engines. Chocolate bar wrappers tended to build up there.

As he'd suspected, it didn't take long before Chief Williams joined him.

"So," Liam said quietly as he shut the cab door and stepped down. "I followed your advice. I got a boyfriend now, everything's sorted out."

Chief Williams didn't look like he was buying it completely, but he nodded slightly. "I've noticed a difference. Okay, son. Just keep out of trouble."

"Yes, sir."

Before the chief could say anything, the bell rang overhead and all thoughts of boyfriends were gone. It was work time.

"That was a nice cool-down run," Chris spoke up as they walked back to the truck together. If they got away with just this call before the last overnight portion of their two days on, Liam would be surprised, but he could always hope.

"Luckily," Liam nodded. As much as they enjoyed the adrenaline, a small fire was always better than the alternative. They'd been here for about an hour. It didn't take long to extinguish the fire that had climbed up the sides of the young family's stove and caught in the wooden cupboards.

Honestly, moving furniture out of the way and checking the walls and cupboards for any residual heat had taken longer than putting out the fire, but it was all important work. Sparks could linger for hours only to reignite with much deadlier consequences.

They took every job seriously, no matter how small the fire seemed to be.

Most of their calls weren't even fires—they were medical emergencies, and it was always a crapshoot what they were going to walk into. In a way, Liam preferred a tiny fire like this.

"Who do we call? What do we do now?"

One of the mothers of this cute young family was showing the kids the engine with Kevin. It was a good educational moment, and it kept the kids' minds off what they'd just witnessed.

That left her wife, a nervous-looking young woman of no more than twenty-four, clutching her cellphone and staring at the ruin in her kitchen.

"I'm leaving our contact information for our fire department contact who can answer any questions later," Liam told her, sinking into the kitchen chair so he was at eye level with her. "Take photos of everything, then call your insurance company right away. They're a good place to start. They'll tell you what they require—normally a walkthrough, possibly with someone from our department. This is a relatively minor incident, thank God. There'll be an investigation to make sure it

E. DAVIES

wasn't arson or something that's your fault, so the insurance will pay out."

"Right." She nodded, chewing the ends of her hair.

"Your insurer will also have some information on fire restoration, how to get the wall and cupboards fixed up. But you won't be replacing everything right away," Liam told her, keeping his voice calm and level. She was slowly relaxing, starting to take notes on her phone. "It takes time for everyone to investigate. Do you have someone nearby to help with cooking?"

"No, yeah, we do," she nodded, looking up at him. "Is it safe to live in?"

"Yes," he told her, "but you'll probably want to keep the kids away from the kitchen so they don't try to taste it."

That made her smile, at least. "Right. Okay. Thank you so much."

With their work done, the only thing left was finalizing the fire report. Liam's gloves and helmet were off by now, so he reached out to shake hands with her. "You're welcome. Our contact details are on that card. If you need anything, get in touch."

"I can't thank you enough."

Now that the need for cool and calm had passed, Liam grew a little flustered when the other woman in the family came over to thank them, along with the kids.

"He's going all shy. I'd better go," Chris finally joked, grinning at Liam as he headed for the engine. "You gonna tell your boyfriend you were a hero today? You should say you had to put out the stove before it exploded and ignited the whole place. Singlehanded. And kicked in the door."

Liam rolled his eyes and laughed with exasperation as he did one last check for leftover gear, then climbed into the cab of the engine. "Like you wouldn't be bragging. Ohhh, that's right.

You can't get anyone to swipe left on Tinder. Or right. Whichever it is." Of all the dating apps, Tinder was one he hadn't tried. Grindr was much too easy and effective.

"Don't kill each other before we get back to the station," Kevin told them, sliding into the driver's seat and pulling down the sun visor.

"I'll do my best." Liam pretended to throttle Chris, but he was grinning as Kevin started up the engine. For his money, any call where they drove away smiling was a good one.

17

LIAM

You can't cook for me. I'm having you over!

Liam leaned on his kitchen counter as he texted Dylan, shaking his head. Therapy was over, but Dylan had another hour left in his shift. He'd been about to start supper, and when he'd texted Dylan to make sure he didn't have any allergies, Dylan had told him not to cook.

Therapy had been easier this week. He didn't feel so much like he was peeling up layers of himself for a stranger to pick through and judge. It wasn't exactly easy still, but his body hadn't thrown flashbacks at him and shut down from stress, either.

Now he knew the term for those weird moments he sometimes had—flashbacks. Gary had taught him that they didn't have to be reliving memories visually, like they were usually shown on TV. They could show up in other ways, like when he couldn't stop shaking, when he'd interpreted accepting sexual attention as wanting it.

You had me over at the station :) My turn.

Liam laughed and rolled his eyes.

I can't believe I'm having you over to cook your own meal. My mom would kill me.

Dylan just sent a kissing emoticon and a wink, and Liam snorted with laughter.

Fine LOL. At least let me get groceries. Need anything?

Do you have food in your kitchen?

Liam laughed again and went to crash on the couch with his phone.

Of course.

Then I'll find something. Gotta go work. See you soon. xox

Liam shook his head and sent back a quick *xox* to Dylan before he put his phone away. Even via text message, Dylan was strong-willed. It was one of the things he liked about him.

"In that case..." He hauled himself off the couch again to tidy up the living room, making sure his little apartment was straightened out.

It was hardly a big place—a one-bedroom, in fact—but it was his own, and it was gorgeous. He loved the hardwood floors and the airy windows, the little Juliet balcony, the kitchen island, and the ceramic bathroom floor. It was breezy in the summer, which helped keep it cool, and the corner location meant he got plenty of light even in the winter.

Not that winter here was anything like Boston. Every now and then, he missed the pretty first snow falling on the historic buildings downtown, but that got old after the first two or three snowfalls. No more digging their way to hydrants or medical calls for slip-and-falls on steep, icy driveways.

Instead, they had wildfires. Oh, well. Win some and lose some.

At last, there was a knock on the door and he cast one more quick look around the room, then strode to answer it and let Dylan inside.

"Hey." His date looked adorable—had he run home to

change? He was in a different shirt now, a dark navy collared shirt with a yellow floral pattern.

"Hi. Looking good," Liam told Dylan with a smile. He was a little embarrassed he hadn't thought to change since therapy, since he hadn't been doing any deep cleaning on the house—just tidying. Fire station etiquette had him well-trained in staying up-to-date with the other chores.

"So are you, handsome." Dylan stepped inside and rested his hand on Liam's chest, leaning in for a kiss but letting him close the gap.

Liam appreciated that little gesture of consideration. He didn't even feel a thrill of nerves through him as he pressed his lips against Dylan's. They were warm and familiar now.

Dylan's chest brushed his as he leaned in, then pulled back again and smiled softly. "How'd it go this week?"

There was no doubt what he meant. "Better," Liam admitted, following Dylan toward the kitchen. "I'm a lot calmer this time. There's a lot of logically thinking through stuff."

Like when Gary had asked him to think about why he was throwing himself into sex. As strange and uncomfortable as it was to admit it to himself, he'd realized that it was an adrenaline rush. Not always in a good way, but one nonetheless. That had gotten him thinking: maybe he'd wound up in his job because he needed that rush as often as he could get it.

"I'm glad you're finding it's helping," Dylan carefully answered. "Can I rummage?"

"Go to town," Liam agreed, pulling up a stool at the island. He watched as Dylan pulled out ingredients: pasta, spinach, tomatoes, and cream, then spices. "You're cooking without a recipe?"

"Yep! It's my favorite thing to do," Dylan admitted. "Like those cooking shows."

Liam grinned. "You want me to challenge you? Throw in, like, a peach and some obscure type of fish?"

"No!" Dylan laughed. "I want to make something that actually tastes good."

"I have wine," Liam offered, pushing his hand back through his hair. "White or red."

"A light red? Acidic?"

"Aye-aye, sir," Liam teased as he got up to check his wines. He kept a few bottles around for those of his friends with an actual palate, or dates, or, ashamed as he was of it, those rare nights alone in front of the TV where he needed one.

He found something that fit the bill and opened it while Dylan cooked the pasta. It only took minutes before his kitchen was smelling good.

When he spotted his chance to help—by chopping tomatoes—he pulled up a chopping board and did just that while Dylan stirred the sauce.

Dylan paused in front of the stove after he turned off the pasta water to peck his lips, then murmured, "Out of the way. Don't want to burn you."

Liam saluted and stepped back as Dylan poured out the boiling water.

Every time they brushed by each other, even accidentally, Liam shuddered. It wasn't an unpleasant shiver, but now that he was aware of it, it was distracting. On one level it was pleasant: his skin crackled with the sexual tension, the pent-up heat between them. On another, he was aware now of the rush of blood to his head. The electric jolt felt like glancing down from the edge of a building.

"And we're just about there," Dylan finally announced with a smile at him. They were about halfway through the bottle of wine now, chatting about their days at work. A nice, safe topic.

"I'll set the table."

Liam had picked up a few fake flowers from the shop, regardless of how much Vee teased him for it, and a little vase. He had that on the table already, but he added placemats, utensils, and their wine glasses. He opened the Juliet balcony doors so they could get a breeze through the place.

Dylan carried over their dishes of pasta and the salads Liam had thrown together from what he had on hand, then settled at the table opposite him.

It was hard not to stare at Dylan while they chatted about little things—the knitting group, which he'd finally be able to go back to next week, and a prank Chris had played on Kevin last week. The whole time, Dylan was smiling at him, paying attention to everything he said like it was equally important.

That feeling was back: open air in front of him. He wasn't thinking straight, and his foot slipped off the edge. "I'm really attracted to you."

Instantly, the panic set in—not a flashback, though. Nothing more than normal romantic nerves. *Fuck. Why did I go and say that?*

"Me, too," Dylan said. He pushed back his empty dinner plate and picked up his wine glass, cradling it in his palm as he watched Liam. "But I don't want to push you."

Liam let a quick sigh escape as he straightened up and mirrored Dylan's move. "You won't," he promised. "I've... done a lot of things with a lot of people."

"Ooh. You playboy," Dylan teased, his tongue stuck out just slightly between his lips.

Liam grinned and rose from the table, waving his hand at the dishes to indicate they could leave them. He'd wash up after Dylan left. Instead, he led Dylan over to the couch, next to the balcony doors, still carrying his wine glass.

Dylan sat gingerly next to him and turned to face him,

bracing his elbow on the back of the couch and the side of his head on his fist. "So... You're not just trying to hook up with me?"

"No," Liam murmured, frowning.

Dylan glanced at his expression, then tilted his head. "That's a bad thing?"

"No! No, not at all." Liam had to try to get his words in order before he fucked this up. He hadn't had a relationship discussion since... well, since his last ex, and look how that had gone. "I'm just not used to it."

"If you want to make out for like an hour, I can do that," Dylan offered frankly, a grin spreading across his face.

That made Liam laugh, and it broke the tension between them for a moment.

Liam shifted his wine glass into the other hand to drain it and set it aside, then slowly ran his hand up Dylan's thigh toward his hip. "I'd really like that. I was thinking of more, actually."

"Oh?" Dylan breathed out. He set aside his glass and shifted on the couch, swinging his knee over until he straddled Liam's lap. He sat back on Liam's knees, playing with the hair at the back of his neck and holding on loosely as he grinned. "Like what?"

"A little of this, a little of that..." Liam winked.

He didn't mind this. He was a bit jittery, but he felt confident and in control. He'd done this a million times. Well, not a million, but definitely more than he'd admit to anyone else. There was no reason to be nervous now.

And he wasn't even nervous about the idea of sex with this gorgeous, clever, genuine guy who'd ended up in his lap. It was just...

"Ah," he murmured quietly to himself.

"Mmm?"

"I haven't had a date where we *didn't* end up fucking in... um..." Dylan was pretty good at not raising his brow, but even he probably would. "A while," Liam finished with a laugh.

Dylan's eyes sparkled. "I'd rather not rush it, then. I would *love* to suck you off, though," he said. His voice trailed off into a low moan of desire.

Liam's fingers tingled with warmth, his cheeks flushing. He reacted on impulse, pulling Dylan in for a long, slow kiss. At least, it started off slow.

Within seconds, Liam was running his hands down Dylan's back, enjoying the firm warmth of the body against his. Dylan spread his knees so he could press closer, their chests and stomachs and thighs rubbing as his bulge pressed into Liam's hip.

Dylan's hand ran up his side to his shoulder, then cupped his cheek. The warm, affectionate touch stilled Liam's shiver, and made his eyes slide closed.

With Dylan, he felt safe.

"I would kiss you forever," Dylan whispered, brushing his lips along Liam's jaw to his ear. His warm, open-mouthed kiss just below Liam's ear made him shiver, but this was pleasant.

"Hnnh," Liam managed in response, his nails digging into Dylan's back. He caught his breath when Dylan's tongue flicked along his earlobe. "*Fuck.*"

"You're sensitive there," Dylan murmured into his ear with one more kiss behind it, then kissed along his throat. "Where else are you sensitive?"

"All... over," Liam murmured back. He was busy unbuttoning his shirt to loosen it enough that he could yank it up, over his head.

Dylan helped him fight his shirt off his wrists, then sat back to run his hands down his muscled frame. Liam grinned at Dylan's hungry expression. There was no doubt he found him hot. All those workouts paid off now and then.

"You probably hear it all the time," Dylan waved a hand when Liam looked at him expectantly. "I won't go there."

"Oh, but not from *you*," Liam teased. "Go on."

Dylan clicked his tongue. "Fishing for compliments?" He slid back on the couch, bending to lick until he had Liam's nipple in his mouth. "Naughty."

"I—fuuuck." Liam's curse turned into a moan as his cock throbbed. He was hard in his pants now, his toes curling into the ground as he spread his legs and pushed up into Dylan's body. Dylan's hand was running down his stomach to his pants to grab his dick and squeeze.

His body burned with need, and he pushed his hips up into Dylan's palm. Usually he took charge in moments like these, grabbed the other guy's hand, got him to squeeze his cock while he whispered something dirty about how he was gonna feel it inside him.

But not with Dylan. Liam let Dylan rub with his palm, then two fingers curling around the shaft to stroke it from outside his pants.

"Can I—" Dylan started.

"You better," Liam laughed breathlessly, rolling his head back to stare up at the ceiling as Dylan's tongue flicked out to caress the nub of flesh. "Fuck..." He was gonna come in his pants if Dylan kept rubbing him like that. He worked his hands under Dylan's shirt to run up his bare back. "Jesus Christ."

Dylan laughed warmly and unbuttoned his jeans, then unzipped them. He kept mouthing at Liam's nipples. "I brought condoms."

"Good. Mine are... somewhere," Liam waved lazily toward his bedroom. He couldn't spare the syllables to elaborate. He was moaning quietly with each flick of that skilled tongue and suck of those pursed lips. His nipples were usually sensitive, but so was the rest of him under Dylan's light touches and soft palms.

And Dylan's hot mouth, which was finally kissing down from his nipples along his abs as Dylan ran his tongue along each one.

He grunted and pushed his hips into Dylan's palm, which had gone still on his throbbing erection. He was going to have to get out of his underwear.

Dylan flicked his hands away when he tried to push his boxers down, and Liam groaned in protest, running his hands through Dylan's hair instead.

"I'm getting there," Dylan chuckled deeply, kissing just under his belly button.

So fucking close it hurt, but Dylan was only getting started. Dylan's kisses were muted by hair and fabric until they pressed along his shaft, through cloth.

"Oh, *fuck*." Liam let go of Dylan's head so he didn't just shove him down onto his needy cock. His head spun, his stomach tight already as his body pulsed with rhythmic throbs of heat. He needed to be in Dylan—in his hand, at least, or his mouth, or his tight little ass.

He could picture Dylan riding him hard and fast, sweaty and naked on him, and holy fuck, if that wasn't the best visual he'd ever seen.

"You're so damn hard," Dylan whispered, mouthing at the cloth-covered bulge. He found the head and pressed his tongue against the underwear. The warm, slightly damp pressure wasn't nearly enough against the throbbing skin.

"Fuck," Liam mumbled, squeezing his eyes shut before he couldn't resist looking down again. Dylan was on his knees between his legs now, his thumbs hooking into Liam's underwear. Liam gladly arched off the couch to let Dylan pull his underwear down past his knees, then stepped out of it and rubbed Dylan's shoulders. One hand cupped the back of his neck.

Dylan pulled back to grab a condom and rip it open, and then he sucked the tip into his mouth. One hand wrapped around the base of Liam's cock. He pressed his open mouth around Liam's shaft and slid it down, rolling the condom down with his mouth and lips.

Liam hissed his pleasure at the wet, tight heat suddenly around him and swallowed his gasp as Dylan slid his lips down to the base of his cock, then back up again.

Dylan moaned his agreement, his hand squeezing Liam's shaft and twisting slightly with each downstroke, his lips tight against his fingers, everything *so* fucking tight around Liam's dick...

"I'm gonna come so fast," Liam laughed breathlessly, but he couldn't look away. Never mind his fantasy—*this* was the hottest thing he could imagine. Dylan, right here on his knees, sucking his cheeks in around him. Those thick, pretty lips stretched around his shaft. Green eyes gazing up at him.

Dylan slid his other hand up Liam's stomach, idly feeling him up, until his fingers brushed the nipple.

Liam nearly saw stars. His head slammed back so fast he bumped the wall behind the couch, his nails biting into Dylan's shoulder as his other hand dug into his own thigh. "*Fuck!*"

With just a few more bobs of Dylan's head, a few more swirls of Dylan's tongue around the head of his cock, he came so hard he lost his voice. He gasped Dylan's name silently as the heat crashed through his body, pleasure all he could see, feel, or taste. The hand and mouth around his cock were all he could feel, his hips thrusting instinctively to push into Dylan's mouth a few last times.

He was warm and wet and tingly when he came down, his cock softening and his vision clearing up a little. The back of his head ached slightly, but Dylan's hand instantly came up to rub it as Dylan pulled his mouth off his shaft and kissed the center of his chest. "You okay?" Dylan murmured, concern in his eyes.

"Fuckin' *great*," Liam laughed breathlessly, touching Dylan's hand on his head, then bringing it down to his lips to kiss his fingers for the sweet move.

"Okay," Dylan laughed. He sensed that he wanted him to get up, and he rose. Liam pulled him over his lap.

"You're still too dressed," Liam complained, plucking at Dylan's shirt. He could feel Dylan's cock pressing into his leg now. Dylan was being surprisingly restrained about it, but Liam wanted to do something for him.

"Sorry," Dylan grinned. He unbuttoned his shirt from the top while Liam ran his hand up from the bottom, waiting impatiently until he could touch all that bare skin.

He was gorgeous. Not hunky and muscled like Liam or the other guys at the station, but soft and tender. Liam could faintly feel abs under his soft, smooth belly when he ran his hand up, but that was it.

God, he wanted to spend a night kissing him all over.

For now, Liam shifted carefully to lie down along the couch, encouraging Dylan to kneel over his chest.

Dylan hesitated, and his eyes widened. "Are you sure?"

Liam had never been more sure of anything. His chest was thumping with excitement, not nervousness. Once he got *into* sex, he was just fine. It was just beforehand that the adrenaline struck... especially with strangers.

Dylan? He trusted Dylan. He *wanted* Dylan.

With Dylan's jeans down, he admired his tight briefs for a moment before hauling them down, too. The pink, firm shaft that bobbed in the air looked delicious.

"I like the view," Dylan hummed as he looked Liam up and

down, still kneeling over his waist. The couch barely had room for them both at this angle, but he kept one elbow on the back of it to steady himself.

Liam grinned at the way Dylan's eyes wandered over his body, his cock twitching once. "I'm afraid I can't put condoms on with my mouth the way *some* mad-talented people can."

"I'll survive," Dylan laughed as he rolled the length down his shaft, then licked his lips. "Should I just...?"

Liam grabbed Dylan by the hips to encourage him to crawl forward and lean over him, then closed his hand around that warm, thick shaft and stroked it a few times as he brought his mouth to the tip.

"Oh, fuck." Dylan mumbled, then hissed a breath in when Liam closed his mouth around the tip. The condom barely tasted like anything, so Dylan's smell was still forefront in his nose as he bobbed his head slowly down, sucking his cheeks in around the shaft.

Dylan's moans were their own reward. He had one hand firmly curled around the arm of the sofa next to Liam's head, and the other was around the back of the sofa to steady himself.

Liam took the length in until his lips met his fingers, swirling his tongue around the length and rubbing his tongue around the head as he came back up. With each bob of his head, he let the wet noises and tightness do their work on Dylan.

"Oh, God. You're good," Dylan mumbled, his body flinching and quivering when Liam's tongue tapped the underside of his dick. "Fuck..."

Until Dylan pulled back, Liam thought that watching his careful composure come apart as he writhed above him with pleasure was the best part of all.

Then he changed his mind.

The best part was when Dylan moaned, "Can I come on you?"

"Mmmhmmm," Liam drawled, drawing out each sound so it felt good around Dylan's cock.

Dylan scrambled to slide back on the couch until he was straddling his hips again, yanked off the condom, and started jerking himself off.

Holy fuck, Liam changed his mind once again. *That* was the hottest thing he'd seen. Dylan's hand pumped up and down his shaft as he twisted his wrist at the end of each stroke. His lips were parted, his cheeks flushed and head rolled to the side a little. His eyes raked up and down Liam's body, from his softening cock along his thigh to his biceps—built with real work, not endless curls.

"Oh, God, yes," Dylan moaned when Liam reached out to give him a hand, letting go of himself so Liam could stroke. He grabbed Liam's shoulder with one hand and the back of the couch with the other, his knees digging into the sofa as he thrust into Liam's hand.

Liam only had to jerk his hand along that hardened cock a few more times before Dylan gasped, his eyes widening and nails digging into Liam's shoulder.

"Fuck, I—Liam!"

"Come on, baby," Liam purred, licking his lips as he squeezed and stroked the warm, velvety weight. His thumb was wet with the liquid already trickling from Dylan.

He was rewarded with a throaty gasp, and then Dylan clenched and shuddered and came hard, shooting across his chest and stomach and hissing out curse words.

Liam raised his hand to rest on Dylan's side and make sure he wasn't going to tip over when his muscles relaxed, but his whole body was still flushed with heat. He loved this view of

Dylan more than anything—his face taut with pleasure, his abs clenched and thighs quivering.

In the back of his mind, he wondered if Dylan would look like this when he rode his cock.

"Oh, wow," Dylan moaned as Liam let go of him and rested his hand on his stomach, his other hand behind his head. His cheeks were red as he gazed at Liam. "Fuck, I'll get you a… tissue. Hold on."

Liam laughed and let Dylan grab some from the tissue box, but his chest was warm. "A hottie like you getting me all dirty? I don't mind," he teased. He took the tissues from Dylan and winked. "You can do it again sometime."

Dylan let out a breathy laugh as he grabbed their condoms and rose to find a bin. "I'd like that a lot."

Liam leaned over to watch that ass disappear around the kitchen corner, grinning when Dylan looked at him. "I have some other ideas, though," Liam winked.

"Oh, me too." Dylan was definitely sauntering back to him, and if he hadn't just come, Liam would swear he was coming onto him.

Liam rose to his feet and pulled Dylan in by the hands, their bodies swaying together naturally. As soon as he let go of Dylan's hands, their hands snaked around each other's shoulders and waist, pulling close as their lips met.

He didn't usually kiss his hookups afterward. There was no sexual intention here, just… affection and tenderness. It was the oddest feeling, and he didn't know what to do with it.

This was the opposite of the adrenaline rush he usually found himself compelled to seek. This was softness, security, and understanding.

The stress was building like an itch under Liam's skin, accompanied by anxiety. Hugging Dylan and being physically close to him helped, but he had to take a deep breath to get it under control.

Sex was the only way he usually blew off that steam when it built up, but that was out. It had been weeks since he'd fucked anyone, and Liam was starting to feel it. Blowjobs helped a little, but the animal part of him that wanted to just mindlessly lose himself... it was hard to keep it on a short leash.

Dylan's eyes were closed, but when Liam peeked through his lashes, he was smiling through the kiss.

"Mm," Liam murmured under his breath, pulling back enough that their noses brushed but their lips were just apart. "That was good."

"It's not triggering?"

"No. Just the beginning was," Liam murmured, his arms sliding down to loosely hold Dylan around the waist. "I think. I haven't practiced picking it out, exactly. But that felt really good."

Dylan smiled, those warm green eyes open now and gazing into his own. "Good. And you're not doing me and ditching me."

"No drive-bys," Liam promised, then patted that firm ass and grinned. "I wanna take my time."

Dylan wiggled his head playfully as he pulled back from Liam, making Liam chase another peck on his lips. He pecked Liam back, then bent over to grab his clothes. "Oh, you'd better."

It took them a minute to sort out their clothes, though Liam left his own off since he was about to grab a shower.

"I'd better get going, huh?" Dylan smiled. "You look wiped."

"Sorry," Liam apologized. The day after his shift ended was always a short one. He napped in the morning and then tried to push through the full day before sleeping. It was a struggle by evening, though.

Dylan shook his head. "No, it's all right. I've got my first day of class tomorrow, anyway."

Liam brightened up. He'd almost forgotten that Dylan's classes were already beginning. "Right! You want me to drive you there?"

Dylan looked nervous, but he shook his head again. "I think I'll be okay for one day. They don't say anything important on the first day. We'll walk around the campus on the weekend."

"Sounds like a plan," Liam murmured, pulling Dylan in for one more soft kiss. "Sleep well, then."

As he saw Dylan off, Liam's chest still felt tight. He'd gotten through this just fine, like he had gotten through a hundred dates—and hookups—before this. It made him frown as he hit his bed minutes later, getting an early night.

If the blowjobs had been great and the romance warm afterward, what was wrong?

He was only good for sex. He was going to be a terrible boyfriend. A couple of weeks without one specific kind of sex couldn't be this big a deal for most people. Why him? He had his job for adrenaline, and Dylan for cuddling, even orgasms. Surely that was enough.

Not good enough for me, apparently. I'm fucking terrible. This is why my last ex left me in Boston, the voice in the back of his head reminded him. He shut off the light and rolled over, focusing on mentally rehearsing turnout drills until he fell asleep.

18

DYLAN

You sure you're ok?

Dylan smiled as he read Liam's sweet text. He was in his car, having managed to find a campus parking spot he was allowed to use. He'd ordered his textbooks online so he could save money and avoid the campus bookstore, and he had the books with him for his two classes today.

He'd gone to class hundreds of times during his associate's degree, but never here. Only at the community college, with its gorgeous green overlooking the water and small, friendly buildings.

This was a whole different ball game. The campus stretched out seemingly endlessly. He'd heard plenty of rumors about the campus from friends—that some people had to bike around it, that sometimes freshmen got assigned classes that were impossible to be on time for because they were too far apart.

Dylan hoped all that space meant it wouldn't feel crowded in the fall.

He answered Liam's text.

I'll be fine xox.

It wasn't strictly true. He was already feeling tense and fearful, his stomach too nervous to eat. He hadn't eaten all morning, either.

But Dylan had to push through. He'd gotten better already, or he would never have been able to go to the community college. He reminded himself of that fact several times before he got the nerve up to unbuckle his seatbelt and climb out of the car.

His mother had been more than useless when he'd texted that morning to remind her that it was his first day at UCSB. She'd answered a while later to remind him to ground any negative energy.

"Fine," Dylan snorted and took a deep breath, imagining his anxiety sinking out of his body into the ground.

It didn't work. His shoulders sank a little and his heart slowed, but his muscles were still tight. He swallowed hard and grabbed his backpack, then locked the car.

He'd picked a spot relatively close to the building where his psych classes were held. It was only a short walk across campus, and the small crowds of students his age didn't make him nearly as nervous as kids did.

That was still kind of sad when he thought about it, but he tried not to.

Dylan managed to find his way to the building without further issue, mostly by thinking about everything except where he was and who was around him. The halls weren't crowded, but he'd arrived a good few minutes early.

He found a chair outside the classroom to sit in and grabbed his phone to scroll idly through his messages with Liam, distracting himself.

"Hey, man. You here for Psychology of Emotions?"

Dylan dragged his attention off his phone and looked over

at the guy who'd dropped into the seat next to him. "Yeah. You?"

"You bet. I'm Rod." Dylan took one glance at Rod and almost made a face. That hideous plaid shirt and khaki shorts? Worse yet, socks and sandals? Definitely straight. At least he was talking to him unprompted.

Be grateful for that, Dylan scolded himself and sat up straighter. He knew how to make conversation. "Hi. Dylan. I just transferred here for Summer Start, from the community college."

"Oh, sweet. Good for you," Rod nodded. "I've been here since freshman year. Yeah, I had to repeat a year, so I'm a nontraditional student." He wore his baseball cap backward. He took it off and put it back on again, smoothing down his hair underneath.

Dylan bit back his amusement. No, *he* was a nontraditional student—admitted to the community college at twenty-one for his first year, after his failure to complete even a semester the first time around.

But hey, he didn't know Rod's circumstances. "Yeah? Me too. Got started late."

"Here's to late bloomers." Rod fist bumped him and grabbed his bag. "So you got the new textbook?"

"No." Dylan frowned, worry clawing at his stomach as people started to crowd closer to the door, waiting for the previous class to finish before they headed inside. He focused on his new friend instead.

"Good. Don't waste your money. There's not even a stupid access code or anything."

"Seriously?" Dylan snorted. "Yeah, I got all my books online. I've been round the block."

"Smart man. I'm keeping you around for pop quizzes," Rod

pointed at him with an easygoing grin, and Dylan smiled back. "So, Pysch major? BA or BS?"

"Arts."

"Me too. Fuck that biopsych shit. Science labs? I didn't go to school to be stuck in labs all night," Rod rolled his eyes expressively.

Dylan smiled to himself. Labs didn't actually sound that bad to him, but he'd picked Arts before he'd been confident in himself that he could do this.

The doors opened and students flooded out from the last lecture.

Dylan hissed and dug his fingers into his knees as people started brushing past his knees, their bags bumping his arms and even his face. He leaned back in the chair.

"Rude, I know." Rod swatted away any purses that almost hit him. "You all right?" He was looking at Dylan weirdly.

Oh, come on. Don't freak out on someone new. Dylan drew a deep breath and let it out. "Just don't like crowds."

"Oh, you're one of those... uh, I forget what it's called."

"I'm not agoraphobic, if that's the one you're thinking." Dylan smiled slightly. "Just don't like them."

"Fair enough, man. I used to hate spiders. You know, like everyone ever." Rod stood up, waiting for the last few people to pass by before heading for the classroom. "I trained myself out of it."

Dylan raised his brows and hurried after Rod. "No therapy or anything?"

"Nah. Don't need that shit. I mean, that'll probably be my future career or whatever, I shouldn't dis it, but..." Rod waved a hand.

Dylan shrugged. "Nah, fair enough." He hadn't exactly had great therapy experiences. The year of therapy that *had* worked out well for him before their insurer stopped covering the therapist had gotten him from homeschooling to college, but that was it. Other therapists didn't get it, or tried to get him to do stupid exercises.

He wasn't traumatized, exactly. He had some memory loss, yeah. Didn't like thinking about parts of his childhood. That didn't mean he was *broken*.

"You live nearby?"

"Yeah, I'm in a frat house on Isla. You ever think about rushing one, talk to me, I'll get you in," Rod grinned. "Ours is the best."

"Obviously," Dylan teased, grinning as he slid into a seat in the lecture hall next to Rod. "I bet they all say that, too."

"Yeah, but it's *true*."

Focusing on just one person made it easier to ignore the number of students filing into the classroom around them until their professor came in, and he had one person to focus on throughout the lesson.

Maybe I can do this after all.

"Shit," Dylan whispered as he slammed the stall door shut. He'd barely made it out of the classroom and into the men's bathroom next door without dry-heaving. His first class had gone well, lulling him into a false sense of security.

Then, the second class. It had been in one of those stupid rooms with the desks crowded close together, and he'd found himself surrounded by a group of friends who knew each other from some other class.

It was stupid. That, of all things, shouldn't set him off. He should have looked up, smiled, made friends with them.

Instead, he'd kept his head down and not said a word for the whole class, focusing all of his attention on writing notes and doodling in the margins. The professors in both classes had started teaching instead of doing a syllabus review, which caught him by surprise. Thank God he hadn't tried to skip the classes.

And on the way out of the room, he'd gotten trapped between clusters of students waiting to talk to the professor.

Now he was almost puking in the bathroom?

He sank to sit on the toilet, his head in his hands as he counted down from ten. Then he started looking around, forcing himself through his little exercise.

Look at five things.

The white tile floor, gray walls around the cubicle, the toilet paper dispenser, the hook on the back of the door, and the flickering lights overhead.

What was another sense? Smell. Ew, he didn't want to smell four things, but he did.

By the time he worked down to the single taste—mint from his toothpaste that morning—he almost had his heart rate under control.

He just had to get home. And do this three times a week.

It occurred to him a moment later that he could wait until the next class was in and avoid at least half the crowds, which gave him a great excuse to hide in here for a few minutes more while he pulled himself together.

At least he had one buddy in class, and both classes themselves had seemed easy but enjoyable.

He *liked* what he learned. He just didn't like having to be around all these other people to do it.

And yet I like people. Dylan drew a breath and let it out.

Maybe he should get into therapy like Liam.

A second later, he almost laughed. How fucking bad off was he that he wanted to voluntarily get into that situation again? Spilling his guts to a therapist who talked about how it

was normal to be bullied in school and gave him some home-
work about logically considering the situation. CBT was out.
And EMDR, like Gary did? He had to be in a stable emotional
place to do it. He'd never felt like that applied to him.

He finally pried himself out of the stall before people
thought he was doing something weird in there, heading
straight for the parking lot.

As always, he reached out for his keys to dig them into his
palm, letting the sweat on forehead and neck cool as he turned
on the air conditioning for a minute.

He had to get home. There, he could hide from the world
for the afternoon before he had to drive to the shop in the
evening for his shift. And if he were lucky, he could see Liam.

He kept one hand around his keys as he pulled out onto the
road that hugged the beach below, then rounded the circle,
skirting the airport and hitting the highway.

Dylan squinted at the exit sign. How was he already there?
Fuck, wasn't the university ten minutes away on the highway?
He'd missed his exit, but he could take the State Street exit.

Maybe stop by the store.

Velma would know what to say. She always did. Sometimes
it was a hug, and sometimes she told him to get off his ass and
sort out the incoming freight. It always worked.

Wait. Something's wrong.

Dylan sucked in his breath, his thoughts staccato and loud.

There was a car turning in front of him.

He didn't have time to stop.

Only to swerve.

Now there was a telephone pole coming at him.

He closed his eyes, let go of his keys, and hit the brakes.

The sound of crushing metal grated at his ears, tearing
away all his thoughts but one:

Not yet.

19

LIAM

Even through Vee's store's front window, Liam knew the sound of screeching tires, crunching metal and glass.

He was sitting at the table chatting with Velma and a couple of customers, learning the difference between different types of yarns, but he was on his feet without a second thought when he heard that noise.

Pedestrians were recoiling, stepping back and staring, and Liam followed their gazes down the street.

The car now wrapped around a pole was a dinged-up blue hatchback.

His heart leapt into his throat.

It was a good thing the drivers along State Street had pulled over and were rolling down their windows or opening their doors, all eyes on the smoking car, because Liam ran across the street without looking twice. His emotions were too high to remember his training: always watch your surroundings. Don't make yourself a second victim.

But Dylan was in that car.

The relief that flooded Liam's body when the driver's door opened lasted a few seconds. Then his body chilled with fear.

Anything could have happened to Dylan. How fast was he going? What had happened? There was a car parked in the street at cross-angles, the driver already on his phone.

Liam reached the driver's door just as Dylan fumbled with his seatbelt. The desperate relief on Dylan's pale face at the sight of him was matched only by Liam's relief. No blood.

"Don't move. You could have a head injury," Liam breathed out, pushing Dylan's hand away and unbuckling the seatbelt. He slid his hand onto Dylan's chest, keeping him in place. "Did you hit your head on anything?"

Dylan was definitely in shock, his eyes glassy. He was laughing quietly, his hands clutching Liam's. "I'm okay. No."

Liam took a quick glance at the car. It was a write-off. The windshield had crumpled in, bits of glass strewn across the console and passenger seat. The engine was still worryingly smoky, but there was no sign of fire.

"Your neck and back are okay?" Liam confirmed, looking back at Dylan. Pain didn't always set in immediately.

Dylan was pushing to get out, so Liam steadied him, wrapping a hand around the back of his head and neck just in case. He swayed as he stood, but he stood fine, and then he crumpled into Liam, wrapping his arms around him.

A crowd had gathered, but Liam ignored them as he held Dylan close. He was careful not to make any sudden movements, in case he had any strain or whiplash that hadn't yet shown itself.

At the sound of an approaching siren, Dylan jolted, then moaned. "Fuck. Did someone call the cops? What happens now?"

"I'll help you handle it," Liam murmured and squeezed Dylan gently. The driver of the car parked at an angle across the road was stumbling toward them now, looking just as shocked as Dylan.

Liam glared at him but let go of Dylan to let them talk. He took a step back to watch the scene. It was pretty obvious to him what had happened.

"You turned too fast," Dylan breathed out. "Didn't you see me coming?"

"Fuck. No. I thought I had time. Didn't you see me?"

"I had right of way."

Liam gritted his jaw. Dylan was right, but he also knew Dylan had just come from his first day of classes. He might not have been thinking straight. He could have fucking killed himself behind the wheel, right here across the road from the store.

Reality was hitting like a ton of bricks. This wasn't a game —Dylan needed help every bit as much as Liam, or this could happen again. And next time, he could be prying Dylan's lifeless body out of the wreckage with the Jaws of Life they kept in their truck.

That tremble in his body wasn't anything to do with their closeness. It was shock. Liam had seen it in others enough to recognize it in himself. They were both going to need sugar.

"That's the insurance company dealt with for now." Liam looked back over his kitchen island at the couch. Dylan was still sitting where he had been for an hour, wrapped in an extra blanket, curled up with his legs under himself.

Fuck. He'd stopped shaking after the ambulance attendants had told him he *could* skip the hospital after all. Velma had taken them both up to Liam's apartment and force-fed them chocolate, telling Dylan off for the decision not to go to the hospital.

Liam understood the reasoning, even if he wasn't thrilled. Dylan's health insurance should be active now, but he would still have to pay the co-pay. Dylan was clearly uninjured externally, so he was just going to watch Dylan closely this week for any signs of whiplash.

"Thanks," Dylan murmured. He was chewing the side of his thumb, his gaze down on the coffee table.

Liam's heart hurt. "No word back from your mom?"

Dylan shook his head. After a moment, his voice faint, he mumbled, "She doesn't check her voicemail a lot."

Don't curse his mother out. He probably won't appreciate that, Liam told himself. Dylan had called her home phone three times in a row. For a retired woman, she didn't seem to keep in touch with him. Liam just tightly nodded, though, and came to sit quietly next to Dylan for a few minutes.

When Dylan's phone finally went off, they both jolted.

"Hey, Mom." Dylan closed his eyes and leaned back into the couch, wrapping the edge of his blanket around Liam and pulling him in.

Dylan rested his head on Liam's shoulder, and Liam could hear their conversation.

"Are you home?"

"Yes. They told me I don't have to go to the hospital."

His mother's voice was tinny, but even at this volume, it sounded... detached. "Were you having one of your... moments?"

"No," Dylan sighed, his shoulders heaving. "I just had, but I was... okay at that point. He pulled out in front of me. I had to swerve."

"Are you seeing an osteopath about this? Darrell knows a man who treated someone's anxiety."

"Mom," Dylan groaned. "Just once, would it kill you to be like, *I'm sorry, that must suck?* Not *have you tried this alternative medical practitioner?* Jesus."

Liam winced. Anything that could help Dylan seemed worth it right now, but Liam didn't blame Dylan for hating alternative medicine. It was clear that she'd used it, and still did, to avoid parenting.

"If you don't want to see them, all you have to do is say so."

"I don't!" Liam squeezed Dylan's shoulders gently, and Dylan took a deep breath. "I'll keep you in the loop. Gotta go eat. Bye, Mom."

She paused before answering. "I love you. Take care of yourself."

Dylan mumbled, "Love you too," and hung up, then put his phone face-down on the couch and sagged as he let his breath out.

Liam slid both arms around Dylan's shoulders and pulled him in, rocking him gently against him for a few moments. He murmured, "You weren't having... a moment?" He resisted the urge to use the word *flashback.* Dylan was so sure he'd gotten over his childhood beating, but Liam was skeptical. It explained his anxiety around crowds.

Whether or not Dylan was ready for therapy, Liam had the sneaking suspicion he wasn't going to have a choice.

"No," Dylan mumbled. "I was at first. I should've waited to drive. But I calmed down when I was getting off the highway. Then I just... I honestly didn't have time to stop."

Liam believed Dylan if he said that. He rested his chin on Dylan's shoulder. "Okay," he murmured.

Dylan's breathing was quick and shallow now as he straightened up. "How am I gonna get to class? Shit. I can't afford another car. I don't even know if I can drive again. What am I gonna do if I can't drive?"

"Sh, sh," Liam soothed, squeezing Dylan against him until he looked at him. "We'll figure out buses for now. I can drive you in sometimes. It's only three times a week, hm?"

Dylan nodded, looking miserable. "I can't switch to twice a week. I already arranged these shifts with Gary and Vee."

Their closeness helped soothe the burn under Liam's skin, but fuck, it was getting hard not to offer to cheer Dylan up with a quick fuck. *We're not doing that. We're doing it right,* he reminded himself and drew a breath. "Okay," he murmured. Still, he couldn't resist making the offer. Maybe Dylan felt the same. "If you want something to take your mind off it..." he joked weakly.

Dylan smiled, at least, and pressed his lips into Liam's shoulder. "No, thanks. I need to get home and sleep this off. I... fuck. I don't even know the bus routes."

He pulled away and Liam winced. *Fuck me.* For once, that was a curse and not a request. *Now he thinks I'm trying to take advantage of him. And maybe I was.* The more his therapy forced him to think about his own motivations, the less he wanted to.

As much as Liam wanted to be there for Dylan, rejection was probably for the best. Liam didn't want to say or do anything to make Dylan's day worse. "I'll drive you," Liam told him firmly, leaving no room for argument.

They were quiet as they rose from the couch, shedding the blanket. Liam ignored his self-loathing as he grabbed his shoes and keys. He kept arm's length from Dylan as he held the door for him.

Boy, was he going to have an earful for Gary next week.

20

DYLAN

There was no way Dylan wanted to move, let alone check the mail, but the insurance company had said to check the mail for forms they needed him to fill in. Normally Dylan might have left it until a day when he felt more like an adult, but he couldn't fuck this up. If he lost his license, he was going to be in so much trouble.

He'd deflected Liam's attempts to visit him over the weekend, and honestly, it was a good idea on his part. He was a wreck.

Dylan had spent so much time telling himself that it was *just* one little thing that unnerved him, that it wasn't *that* a big deal. He'd carefully constructed his ways of dealing with the panic when it hit, of minimizing and ignoring it, of shoving it to the back of his head.

Dylan wasn't boyfriend material. The realization was like ripping off the bandaid all at once. All he could give Liam was these bits and pieces of him between the darkness. Liam deserved more than that. And he'd told Liam *he* needed therapy? Fuck. He was such a hypocrite. Liam had to see that now.

If the insurance company found him at fault...

He had no idea what would happen then, and he didn't want to know. Visions of being banned from driving and of creditors beating down his door for payments on his tow fees danced behind his eyes when he closed his eyes.

And those were the nice mental images.

He replayed those few seconds—surely to God it had been a couple of seconds, even if it felt like long minutes—over and over.

Maybe, if he'd been more alert, he could have hit the brakes faster.

What if that had happened on the highway?

Would he have wiped out, and taken out someone else?

He could have killed himself and other people.

The rational part of his brain knew that he'd never driven when he couldn't see straight; that he'd done every damn thing he could to keep his attention on the road whenever he felt it was at risk of wandering.

That wasn't the part of him that was winning right now, as he stumbled out to the mailbox near the front of his complex, Monday afternoon. He was forcing himself into class today, one way or another, and getting outside would help him wake up.

Dylan unlocked his mailbox and winced at the sight of a few envelopes, one of them thick and barely stuffed into the slot. The innuendo didn't even make him smile.

He wiggled the stack of mail out and slammed the box shut, then shuffled back up to his apartment.

Another missed call from Liam when he got back into the apartment, where he threw his mail on the table, and poked his cellphone.

He spotted the text.

Do you want me to come over after work?

Oh, right. Shit. Liam was working from today until Wednesday morning. He'd missed his chance to see him.

Which was probably a good thing. Gave Liam some time and space to do what he needed to do.

Dylan wasn't stupid. He knew no guy was gonna hang on and wait for weeks just to fuck him. Blowjobs were nice, but they said *I like you but not that much.*

He was okay, in the vaguest of hypotheticals, with the idea of Liam finding someone else. The actual thought of Liam carrying someone else to his bed didn't make his stomach twist with jealousy.

He'll find someone better than you. He doesn't need to clean up your messes.

Dylan closed his eyes tightly.

"I saw the way you looked at me. I bet you wanted me. Isn't that right, pretty boy?"

Another kick to his ribs, and all he could think to do was shake his head.

"Ewww. Why would I want you?"

Laughter from all around, and jeers.

"Gross!"

That was the nicest thing he heard. He tried to shut out the other words. The pain helped block them out.

He felt sick, but he pushed that down and tore open the envelopes, blinking back the hot tears. This was pretty much the definition of a hot mess. Add a bottle of vodka and he'd be there.

One of the slender envelopes was from the state. Half-expecting an ambulance bill, he was caught by surprise by the contents.

...required by law to send the enclosed form, filled out by a licensed medical practitioner...

Wait, what?

Dylan scanned the letter, and his heart sank so much he had to sit down. He covered his mouth, resisting the bile rising into his mouth.

If he wasn't mistaken, this letter was asking for proof of his medical suitability to drive. Otherwise, his license was going to be suspended.

Who the hell had reported him to the State of California and said he wasn't fit to drive? Who knew about his panic attacks *and* his accident?

Oh. God. No. Say it wasn't Liam.

Dylan's self-pity faded as white-hot anger burned through his body. His breathing shallow, he dug his nails into his palm as he ground his jaw. He picked up his phone and texted back a simple answer.

Yes.

He didn't care if it had been for his own good; Dylan was going to kill him.

21

LIAM

All the guys knew by now that Dylan had been in an accident. Chris was the best about it, not playing pranks on Liam like usual but also not treating him like he was made of glass. After brushing off his chief's concerns by reassuring him that he was ready and able to work without distraction when he was called upon, Liam spent the most time around Chris that Monday.

His weekend had been long. Dylan had only answered his phone once, sounding half-asleep, and he'd barely texted back.

Liam didn't blame him for sleeping off the shock, stress, and fear, but his anxiety mounted as the new week arrived and Dylan still wasn't answering. He wanted to go check on him in person, but he couldn't shake the feeling that Dylan was avoiding him specifically.

"Hey, man." Chris nodded outside. "We gotta wash Betty." Their nickname for engine two was based on a legend of her horn once breaking in the middle of traffic, making her beeps turn into *boop* sounds.

That would give Liam something to do with his nervous energy. Dylan still hadn't answered his question about whether he wanted to see him, and Liam couldn't stop replaying those last few minutes.

Had Dylan seen through his offer of physical comfort as some shallow attempt to get laid? Had that actually been what it was? Liam didn't want to think that about himself, but he wasn't sure.

"Yeah," Liam said automatically, hauling himself off the couch and heading for the garage.

When they had buckets of soapy water, Liam circled around to one side while Chris washed the other. Liam took the street side, mostly ignoring passersby as they ogled the engine— and, no doubt, the firefighters scrubbing it down.

But no matter how much he hated himself for it, the itch hadn't gone away. It had been a long fucking weekend on his own. He'd spent most of his time both days down in the shop with Velma, keeping his mind off the fact that he felt like he wanted—needed—anyone at all.

At least he could pick out the thought pattern better now.

I don't deserve that. "That," of course, being the heart-warming moment between himself and Dylan— the feeling of safety when he was wrapped in Dylan's arms.

A random guy from the street, the bar, or his phone was a risk and a thrill. Maybe he'd let Liam fuck him and it would be great. Maybe he'd hurt him. Liam didn't know which.

Why did he like that? Crave it? Why had it burrowed under his skin until it was all he could think about?

Gary had warned him it would get worse before it got better. Until now, he'd been positive the worst was over, but he wasn't so sure now.

That was before Dylan had ditched him, and before a sexy little blond guy had wandered past the station, looking Liam up and down before looking pointedly at his phone.

His phone went off. Liam had it muted, but he was willing

to bet he knew what app had just sent a notification, making it vibrate.

He waited a minute before he rounded the engine to wash the back, wiping his hands off on his pants before pulling out his phone.

Sure enough, it was a Grindr message.

You look hot washing that engine. Can I wash off your hose?

Heat flooded him, crawling through his chest and up his spine as he closed the app and pocketed his phone.

Christ, he wanted to say yes. To make some excuse to Chris, to sneak the guy into the station somewhere, or even into the engine cab, or follow him around the corner to the gas station bathroom...

I can't let that part win.

Whether or not Dylan was drifting away from him, he'd helped him see that pattern. Hooking up itself wasn't bad— even with a lot of guys.

Doing it from some compulsion to let a stranger hurt him? That was fucked up. He had to put down his foot now.

Liam drew a breath and let it out as he finished up.

They had probably been half an hour working on this, and Chris hadn't said a word. It finally occurred to him that it was kind of weird for him. That would give him something to think about other than his dick, at least. As he hosed off the soap, he called to Chris to get out of the way so he didn't splash him.

When Chris came up beside him, Liam glanced at him. "You had an okay weekend?"

He didn't miss the wince that crossed Chris's face. "Huh," Chris shrugged casually, grabbing both buckets to dump them out.

"What's up?"

Chris snorted. "Nothing compared to yours."

"C'mon," Liam snorted, turning the hose toward Chris

before flicking it back at the last second. "Don't make me hose you down."

Normally that would get a playful *I don't swing that way* and they'd elbow each other.

Instead, Chris glanced at him a little too fast, his cheeks flushing. "Right. Yeah. It's nothing. Just... someone isn't texting back."

Someone. Not a girl. Now, Liam was interested more than idly. "Uh huh? From Tinder?"

"Yeah." Chris coiled up the hose when Liam shut it off, helping him drag it back into the station. He didn't normally go into *that* many details about his love life, but this was unusually quiet for him, and Liam's suspicion only grew.

"Someone you already met? Or a first date?"

"We went on dates before... and another one this weekend. We swapped numbers again. I said to text me, but... no dice," Chris rolled his eyes. "Whatever. Not my loss."

Liam raised his eyebrows. Chris didn't usually get stuck on a girl that fast.

Chris avoided his gaze for a minute, then snorted and threw the sponges into the empty buckets as he stacked them. "Okay, fine. It was an ex."

"You're trying to get back together with your ex and they're not answering? Dude." Liam looked straight at Chris, folding his arms.

Chris swiped at the back of his neck and glared up at the sun beating down on them, then pulled open the cab door and climbed inside. "Yeah, yeah. I know."

Liam headed into the garage to wait for Chris to back the truck inside, signaling him to stop when he was positioned right, then strolled forward. "You know what I'm gonna say," he told Chris.

Chris blew out a sigh. "I know. But don't worry, man. I'm over it." His tone told Liam he was done with the conversation.

"Right." Liam let it drop, but he eyed Chris again as they walked into the station. There was more than met the eye to his friend, but Chris was not going to share his fucked-up trials and tribulations with him. Most guys just didn't do that.

The chirp of an incoming text message distracted him from thinking about Chris, pulling his attention straight back to his own fucked-up situation.

Yes.

The relief that flooded Liam's body made him close his eyes for a second as he walked into the station. "Oh, thank God." Dylan was going to meet him.

At first, he thought Chris was doing him the world's biggest favor by not asking about his sudden emotional outburst.

The sensations of *cold* and *wet* hit him at almost the same moment.

Liam gasped for breath. He was dripping wet, and Chris was cackling from behind the door. Liam didn't think twice about tossing the empty buckets aside, sprinting after Chris to chase him into the living room.

Laughter broke out through the living room as the guys—Dan, a newly-qualified firefighter doing a tour of the local stations, and Kevin—watched the unfolding fight.

For the first time that weekend, despite being soaked and pissed off, Liam was laughing, too.

"Chris Jameson, you are *dead*!"

22

DYLAN

"Who'd have thought we live right near each other?"

Dylan forced a smile as he looked over at Rod. Of all the obnoxious frat boys in his class, Rod seemed like the most tolerable, and more importantly, Rod both sympathized with his sudden lack of transportation *and* lived close to him.

The clincher was that Rod's first class of the day was the same time as his, so if he hitched a ride with him, he only had to worry about getting the bus back home three times a week. He could deal with that.

"Man, you don't look all right. Are you sure you're fine?" Rod asked, scrutinizing him.

Dylan resisted the urge to tell Rod to keep his eyes on the road every second he was driving, but he curled his hand hard around the door handle. "Uh huh."

It was Wednesday now. Liam's ride home on Friday had been his first time in a car since the accident; Rod had driven him home on Monday, which was the second. This was the third time.

Surely that meant the nervousness would soon fade.

"I don't believe that," Rod snorted. "Look, man. You look better than last night. It's getting better, right?"

Well, when he put it that way... Dylan had barely talked for the ride home on Monday. This *was* an improvement.

"Yeah."

"Exposure therapy. You should do that with crowds. Man, if you rushed..."

"No," Dylan interrupted with a laugh, uncurling his hand from the handle and folding his arms instead. "Not yet."

"At least come out to one of our open parties," Rod offered. "You could use a little fun, right? Who couldn't? We have cheap beer, hot girls..."

Dylan blew out a little sigh. "I guess," he admitted. "The accident, and then..." No, he wasn't gonna whine about his maybe-lover maybe-telling the state that he couldn't drive without being a fucking loser. But he was seeing Liam tonight after class, and he'd pick that bone then.

Rod eyed him. "Boyfriend problems? We have hot guys around, too."

"Uh... something like that." Dylan cast him a quick glance, nervousness clenching his heart. Hopefully he'd judged Rod right.

"That's cool," Rod shrugged. "I don't care who people sleep with. I have a couple gay brothers." Dylan's stomach sank with relief. "But man, that sucks. See? You just need a good party. Come on."

Dylan's smile this time was genuine. It had been too long since he'd gone to one—not since he was a freshman, the first time, and that had been a disaster.

Maybe Rod was right.

"All right," he agreed as they approached the parking lot. "Let me know when and where."

"Sweet!" Rod high-fived him, then parked and jumped out. "Come on, let's make class before we're late."

Dylan was at least smiling as he stuck by Rod's side all the way to the classroom. School was a good distraction for him right now, and Rod was cool. Things could still turn out all right.

23

DYLAN

The moment Liam walked in the door, Dylan was ready with the letter clutched in his hand. He closed the front door, waited for Liam to slip his sandals off, and handed it to him wordlessly.

"Hey," Liam greeted. His brows crinkled with concern as he only got a letter in response, and then he skimmed it. He sucked in his breath. "Wait... Shit."

Dylan's voice was tight. "I don't know who it was, but it can only have been a few people." Already, his resolve wavered. He'd been preparing all day for this—for days, in fact—but Liam's expression was confused enough that he was starting to believe him.

Still, he had to go on.

He drew a deep breath and looked at Liam. "Was it you?"

Liam almost yelped, "*What?*" He stared at the letter again, then looked up at Dylan.

He looked... a little offended, and so hurt. "No."

Fuck. It really wasn't.

Dylan melted, his shoulders loosening as he reached out to touch Liam's arm. "Oh, thank God. I'm sorry."

Liam hesitated to respond. Dylan still held his breath until Liam let out his breath, too, and handed back the letter before pulling Dylan in for a hug. "Shh," he soothed, rubbing his back. "We'll get that sorted out."

"I'm sorry," Dylan mumbled again into his shoulder. "I didn't want to think it was you." How fucking stupid was he? To take the guy who'd been determinedly staying by his side no matter how crazy he was, or his mom was...

He froze. "Oh, no."

"What?" Liam murmured, and then he tensed up. "You know who it is?"

No way would Mom tell them... get in touch with the officials she so hated... right?

But she'd avoided him all weekend. Hadn't called him back when he'd called on Sunday to tell her he was still alive, thanks very much for asking.

And she'd never approved of him not seeking help for his "little problem," as she called it. Of course, they disagreed vehemently on *how* he should get help. If Dylan ever were, he'd talk to a real therapist, not some hokey one like she'd tried to send him to as a kid.

"Mom."

Liam tensed up, but then he nodded slightly. "You think she would?"

"I don't know," Dylan whispered, his throat tight. "But nobody else knew after the accident except you two, Vee... and I know she wouldn't..."

"Agreed," Liam murmured.

"And... I guess, the cops and ambulance guys, but they didn't know about me being... you know, shaky beforehand."

Liam's arms were tight around him, their bodies nestled together as they stood near the front door. The heat from the hard, strong body pressed against his was starting to get to him.

Liam seemed touchy and affectionate, but it was hard not to associate physical touch with the fact that he hadn't gotten laid in fucking *ages*.

And every time Liam's hand ran up his spine, he shivered with the desire to feel that hand on his ass, grabbing him and pulling him closer as they kissed...

Liam seemed like he'd been in a dry spell—at least, before this weekend—from the way he'd tried to hit on Dylan last time they saw each other.

He had to ask, first, though. He couldn't freak Liam out by coming on to him so fast his head spun, like he wanted to. "This is a weird question," Dylan murmured, "but do you want to... I don't know..."

Liam was tensing up now, looking interested as he pulled back from the hug and watched Dylan closely. "If it involves you, me, and being naked, the answer's yes. Especially if it'll help you relax."

"Oof." Dylan grinned. "Yeah, it would."

He was still raw—not physically, but emotionally—from the accident. But closeness helped. Now that Liam was holding him, he remembered how much. He wouldn't want anyone else cradling him like this.

Oh, man. No. He couldn't go having thoughts like that yet. They weren't even unofficially dating. But, on the other hand, it had been a month of dates, making each other laugh and getting to know each other, and they'd only fooled around once.

That sounded serious to him.

Dylan swallowed and pulled back, leading Liam by the hand toward his bed. "I'm sorry the accident got in the way," he murmured.

"Me, too," Liam frowned, squeezing Dylan's hand. He brought his other hand up to rub along the back of Dylan's hand, then up his arm as they stopped by the bed and Dylan sank down onto it.

Dylan scooted back and Liam followed, straddling him to press a gentle kiss on his lips.

"But it wasn't your fault."

Dylan let out his breath and closed his eyes as Liam snaked his arms around his shoulders, squeezing him for a moment. Dylan smiled, resting his cheek on Liam's shoulder and running his hands up his back.

Liam was a little shaky again, but he knew what that felt like now.

He'd still seemed to enjoy himself the last time they were together, so it wasn't a sign to stop. He just had to take it slow until they got into it.

"You wanna get me naked?" Dylan murmured, his eyes glinting as he pecked Liam's lips a few times.

"Oh, yeah," Liam groaned. "I've been wanting that for weeks."

A moan slipped from Dylan's throat as Liam's hands ran up Dylan's body, under his shirt, and then started pulling his clothes away from him.

Rational thought was swiftly escaping him, replaced by pure *need*.

He wanted to forget about the stupid accident, and his own stupidity. About not having a car, and maybe a license, and maybe a functional relationship with his mom. About the self-loathing that had swamped him for days, and the certainty that he'd fuck up things with this gorgeous, sweet guy.

Liam could make him forget about all of it.

He leaned in and pressed his lips against Liam's neck, kissing all the way up to his jaw, then around to his sweet, soft lips.

Kissing him made Dylan only think about *him*, so he did it

a few more times, until their lips slid apart, their tongues teasing each other.

He was out of breath by the time Liam pulled back to yank his jeans off, kissing from his lips all the way down his body to his stomach as he did so.

"Oh, fuck," Dylan whispered, digging his hands into the bed under him and spreading his legs. He had to make sure Liam knew how much he burned for him, his cock hardening already as he squirmed on the bed. "I *want* you."

"I wanna fuck you," Liam whispered back, his lips near Dylan's hip. He kissed it once more, then swooped back up to press their lips together hard.

Dylan kissed him filthily and slow, sucking slowly on Liam's lower lip as he unbuttoned his shirt.

Liam had stopped shaking, and he was intently focused now. He was smiling more, between kisses, and touching more.

Good.

Dylan was glad that he could pull Liam out of whatever place he went to in those first few moments of intimacy. Whatever they had together, it seemed to crack that wall, and then Liam became so much more attentive and warm and playful.

"Thanks for... being patient with me." Liam knelt back, unbuttoning his shirt, and then all Dylan could see were abs, pecs, biceps, and toned, tanned skin.

Holy fuck, Liam was hot.

Liam's unexpected thanks made Dylan's cheeks flush. "Of course! Dude, it's worth... worth waiting. You are. Worth waiting." His eyes were fixed on Liam's hands, which were now unbuttoning and pushing down his jeans.

"All it takes is a little striptease to get you speechless, huh?"

Dylan's cheeks were hot, and he laughed. "Yeah."

"Seriously, though..." Liam kicked off his jeans, and then they were both naked.

Oh, God, Dylan loved this part. It had been weeks since he'd hooked up—a couple of weeks, maybe even a month before they'd met, and *that* was a month ago now.

Shit, he hadn't slept with a guy in that long? Every sign pointed to him being serious about Liam.

That's a mistake I can't make. Nope. Not the moment.

"Mm?"

Liam's voice was low and serious as he cupped Dylan's cheek, scooting back up so their bodies ground together. Their dicks were both hard, and they rubbed as he settled over Dylan, straddling him easily. "It's worth waiting for you."

Dylan closed his eyes, embarrassed pleasure sweeping through him.

"Oh, God, your blush is adorable."

"Shut up," Dylan groaned, smacking Liam's arm.

Liam laughed and pecked his lips. "Won't."

"God. You're obnoxious."

"I am," Liam agreed. "It's a shame you want me so much."

His broad hand wrapped around both their cocks, squeezing them together and stroking.

"Oh, *fuck!*" Dylan moaned. The sensation of hardened skin against skin, velvety warmth teasing at the sensitive spots all along his cock...

He arched off the bed, grabbing Liam's shoulder blades to yank him down and kiss him until they couldn't breathe.

"Mmmph," Liam groaned through their kiss, their lips sliding hard. He thrust his hips once or twice more, forcing the length of his cock past Dylan's until Dylan whimpered.

"Are you... I mean, have you been tested?" Dylan whispered, his voice breaking with how much he wanted to have that man *in* him right *now.*

"God, yes."

"Me, too. I'm fine. Nothing at all."

"Me too."

Dylan's shoulders sank with relief, but he had one more question. He opened his eyes to make eye contact, then murmured, "Have you... fucked other guys since then?"

Liam swallowed hard, and then he shook his head. He looked a little guilty. "I almost wanted to, the other day, and then..." He turned red.

"What?" Dylan prompted, a smile tugging on his lips.

"Nothing," Liam mumbled. "You?"

"I haven't. Not for... a couple months."

They were clear. "You ever bareback?"

"Not... with a guy I don't trust." Liam's eyes were wide now, his cheeks still stained with that blush. "I would with you."

Dylan pulled him in for a long, slow kiss, his hand sliding between them to squeeze around Liam's, which still gripped both their cocks.

"Do it," he breathed out when he finally pulled back, heaving for breath. This heat between them, it was fucking impossible to stop. It was nothing he'd ever felt before. He'd never *wanted* another guy in him without a condom.

It was more than trusting Liam, more than wanting him. It wasn't just lust. It was...

No. Oh, fuck. I'm not good enough for him.

It was never going to work out. Not when he hid in his apartment just because he bumped into a couple of people on campus. But they had *this* moment, right now. If this was the only time they were gonna fuck, he wanted to remember it.

The thought was a punch to the gut. He closed his eyes tightly as he rolled his head back into the pillow. His voice was tight, and he hoped Liam thought it was with pleasure. "Lube's on the bedside table."

"Convenient," Liam teased, kissing his throat. Then, noises: the bed shifting, a crack, and slickness.

And cool, wet fingers around his hole.

"Oh, fuck," Dylan whimpered already, his thighs twitching as he pushed his legs further apart. "Oh, God."

"You're sensitive," Liam whispered, and in his voice was something painfully close to fondness.

He's never gonna stick around. Not once he gets what he wants.

Dylan licked his lips and nodded slightly, then moaned, losing himself in the need to have fingers—no, more than fingers—inside him.

Liam thrust his fingers in and out slowly, the sensitive spot inside him prickling with white-hot pleasure every time he did.

"Fucking hurry up," Dylan moaned, his voice cracking. Liam hesitated, his fingers deep inside Dylan and crooked. The touch to his prostate made Dylan roll his head further back. "Fuck...!"

"You okay?"

Don't let him catch on. Dylan opened his eyes and forced a quick smile. Luckily, his body was burning with arousal, so his hazy stare was easy to interpret as *need*. Not the truth: fear that this new, improved, therapy-adhering Liam was going to walk out that door and never come back to help him pick up his own crazy.

"I will be when you fuck me," Dylan whispered, wiping his arm across his forehead and gasping when those thick fingers slowly pulled out. "Oh, God, yes."

Liam chuckled deeply, the moment passing. He accepted the explanation, and leaned down to kiss Dylan softly.

A thick warmth pressed at Dylan and inside, guided by Liam's hand. Dylan closed his eyes, shuddering with pleasure as he was filled, inch by inch. "Oh, *fuck*."

"Still okay?"

"Mmhmm." Dylan moaned, pulling Liam down into a harder, hotter kiss. He bucked into Liam until Liam grabbed his hip and pushed him down to the bed.

One push of his hips at a time, Liam fucked him slow but deep, and heat rolled through his body. Every time he was filled to his limit and his head spun impossibly with pleasure, Dylan found a new high. Liam's body rubbed along his, and his lips sucked at Dylan's until Dylan yielded and rolled his head back.

Liam dove in, kissing and sucking at his neck as their bodies slammed together faster, harder, better. Dylan was tingling deep within, his toes curling into the bed as it creaked. The more he dug his nails into Liam's back, the more noise Liam made.

"Fuck, Dylan... so *good*," Liam moaned, pressing kisses up his throat. "Oh, fuck."

Dylan had to agree. It was mind-blowing, and not just because he hadn't been pounded into the bed like this in months. Liam's gorgeous body blanketed over his. The heat of his apartment seemed cool now compared to the scorching blaze of bare skin on skin. And that cock hit every right spot inside him, jolting him again. "I'm gonna... L-Liam, I'm so..."

"Me, too," Liam growled, biting his lower lip. His voice was hoarse and rough with sex, and so goddamn hot. He breathed out against Dylan's lips, "Gonna come in you. You want that?"

"*Yes*," Dylan hissed, his thighs quivering as he clenched around Liam unconsciously from arousal at the idea.

That last squeeze was all Liam needed before his breath hitched in his throat. It was his turn to throw his head back as he cried out with desire, his hips shuddering and stuttering.

And, for the first time, Dylan could feel the warmth spilling inside him with each thrust of Liam's hips. It hit nerves he didn't even know he had, made his cock ache with pleasure. He couldn't resist anymore—he reached between them, knocking Liam's arm out of the way, to stroke himself hard and fast.

"*Liam!*" Dylan came so hard he arched off the bed, his chest heaving for breath as blackness closed in around the edges of his vision and the rhythmic shudders of his muscles hit like a tidal wave. He was faintly aware of the moans spilling from his own lips and echoing in his ear from Liam, who still thrust inside in little, sharp movements.

"Oh, God," Liam whispered into his ear. He pulled out, but his body was still so limply draped over Dylan's that his weight pressed him into the mattress. It was hard for Dylan to get his own hand free a moment later.

But Dylan didn't want Liam to pull away. Despite the anxiety clawing at the back of his mind, he didn't feel it in his body for these long few seconds. He was sticky, sweaty, and exhausted, his throat hoarse and his lips dry and aching, but Jesus Christ, he'd never been so satisfied.

His arms were loosely draped around Liam's waist now, his eyes closed as he tried to catch his breath.

Liam was silent, too, his thighs pressing along Dylan's, one hand on his shoulder and the other on the pillow above Dylan's head.

It was the perfect position to kiss him, but Dylan couldn't bring himself to do it. He turned his head away to catch his breath, then shifted a little. The movement prompted Liam to shift, too, and slowly peel himself off Dylan to flop on his side on the bed.

"God, yeah," Liam mumbled, offering a breathless smile.

Everything in Dylan wanted to press close and rub against him, snatch any lingering hormones he could and drink them in like it was all going to be okay.

He drew a deep breath and let it out, then closed his eyes.

After a minute, Liam's hand came to rest on Dylan's side. It was affectionate but not as intimate as it could have been on his cheek or his hip. "What are you thinking?"

"My anxiety's... good right now," Dylan murmured, not opening his eyes yet. "In my body, anyway. Mind's always a different story."

"Good."

"You?"

Liam chuckled gently. "I'm fine," he murmured. "It's still hard sometimes, but... I'm noticing what I do before I do it. I was sexually assaulted as a kid. I don't want to talk about it, because I don't want it to matter to me now, but I want you to know that I'm working on it."

Dylan's chest felt tight. He'd guessed for a while—probably since the first time Liam had flinched when he wasn't even fully aware of it. The confirmation was awful, but Liam sounded... Well, Dylan wished he could feel that way. Liam was going to get through this so well.

"I'm so glad I went for help, even if I didn't think I needed it at the time."

Was that a pointed tone Dylan detected? He cracked his eyes open to peer suspiciously at Liam. The way Liam intently watched Dylan's face, his brows drawn together, told him it was. "Was that about me?"

"Well..." Liam hedged for a second, then drew a breath. Dylan already knew Liam wasn't the type to dance around it when he was directly questioned. "Yes."

"I don't want therapy." Dylan rolled onto his back, Liam's hand slipping off him, and covered his face, rubbing it intently. He couldn't see Liam's reaction, but he heard the quiet, skeptical hum. "I don't."

"I know. It sucks," Liam said quietly. "But your... panic attacks in crowds... are they flashbacks?"

Dylan breathed slowly, digging his nails into his palm.

Liam had no idea how many textbook pages he'd scoured when deciding on that, how many classes he'd applied to himself. He didn't want to lie, though. There was that possibility. He always thought about *that* incident, sometimes replaying it word-for-word. "Maybe."

"And you went through something traumatic," Liam said, his voice level.

Technically, it was a traumatic incident. Dylan's hands were folded on his stomach now, but his eyes were closed. "A bunch of kids jumped me when I was eleven. Usual homophobic bullying stuff, but it got rough. I went to the hospital."

Liam sucked in a breath, and then he hissed a quiet but vehement, "Shit." Dylan shifted slightly, opening his eyes and looking over at Liam. His brows were furrowed with anger, his eyes sad. "I'm... I'm sorry. Wow."

Dylan smiled slightly. "Don't be. Everyone says that. I don't like talking about it. Like you said, I don't want my life to be all about that, even if that's all it seems to be these days."

"Yeah." Liam reached out slowly, as if to give Dylan a moment to push him away, before he rested his hand on Dylan's shoulder. "You didn't deserve that. But man, I didn't know it was that bad. If you're having flashbacks and panicking still... you need to get help so you're not hurt more someday."

Dylan felt sick as he sat up and pushed himself off the bed, heading to the bathroom to clean himself up. "I've thought about it."

After a few moments, Liam followed. He came up behind Dylan and grabbed a washcloth to clean up. "With Gary?"

"Shit, I don't know." Dylan hadn't meant to snap, but it came out that way. He tightened his jaw.

Liam pressed, "Soon? You need to talk to someone."

That was not what Dylan wanted to hear. He turned and

strode for the bed, grabbing his underwear to slip back on. "I'm *fine*."

"No, you're not." Liam was watching him levelly in the mirror, the washcloth in the laundry bin now. He backed off to give Dylan some space, heading back to the bed to get dressed again. As he sat on the edge, he looked up at Dylan again, though. "Not if you're crashing your car."

That was a low blow. "That wasn't because... no. He turned."

"You weren't distracted at all?"

Dylan knew it was stupid before the words were out of his mouth, but he couldn't help it. "You're sure you didn't slip up and report me? It's sounding a lot like you did."

Though he was clearly irritated, Liam held back and calmly raised his eyebrows as he buttoned up his jeans. "I don't lie. I'm just saying... it's a weak spot, and you don't have to deal with it alone."

Weak. I'm not fucking weak, I'm just... broken. And that's not what he deserves, is it? He's dealing with his shit, and I can't even talk to my own boss about it. "You know, I should get to bed," Dylan stated flatly.

Liam nodded, silently buttoning up his shirt. His eyes were down, resigned to something or other. He didn't even try to argue with Dylan. Once he was dressed, he padded over to the door and slipped his sandals on. "I... I think I gotta miss therapy tomorrow. Chris wanted me over."

"Okay." Dylan kept his voice carefully neutral. He stayed by the kitchen counter, his arms tightly folded. The pleasant buzz in his body was gone now, and his eyes stung. *Just get out so I can cry this out, damn it.*

He looked away from Liam until the door opened and closed. Dylan barely made it to the still-rumpled bed before he collapsed on it.

Well done, the self-critical voice whispered to him. He'd just fucked up his only solid, mature, stable relationship. He couldn't even keep one good thing around. At least he'd cut this off cleanly, before words like *boyfriend* started to get used. Liam was gonna give up on him sooner or later—might as well be now.

Tears flooded him as he pressed his face into his pillow, letting himself melt into it. At last, the numbness was gone; it had melted into something much sharper that tore at his heart until he gasped for breath.

He'd rather have been numb again.

24

LIAM

"You're seriously going in on your day off tomorrow? You softy. Heads."

Liam reflexively reached up to grab the beer can Chris threw at him before it glanced off his head. He flipped his friend off, then cracked it open and sipped, sprawling in his lawn chair. "Only for the morning. It's the last school trip of the year," Liam grumbled. "I don't wanna miss that one."

They were sitting in Chris's backyard, watching the barbecue heat up. Liam's stomach growled as he waited. He had been eating all day, but he still wasn't satisfied.

And he kept getting Grindr messages—offers that made him queasy, but were almost impossible to pass up.

It had been a long fucking day.

Liam could use another six-pack to himself, but he wasn't going to get himself hungover before presenting fire safety to a bunch of rowdy nine- and ten-year-olds.

"Fine," Chris raised his hands. "Be a total nerd. I'll come in if you want the help."

"See? Now who's a softy?" Liam wagged his beer can at Chris. "I knew it."

Chris rolled his eyes. "Fine," he agreed, which told Liam that Chris knew he was going through a tough spot. That, and his reluctance to joke around like usual.

Liam had spent enough damn time today thinking about Dylan and the strange rollercoaster that yesterday had been. From his excitement to see Dylan to surprise and worry at his reception, then sympathy for Dylan's mental state. Excitement, tentative pleasure at finally getting closer to Dylan. Pride in himself for noticing and distracting his mental patterns.

And then he'd pushed Dylan much too hard, and Dylan had put his foot down. They'd barely looked at each other in that last minute.

That *couldn't* be the last time they saw each other. Liam couldn't stand the thought of leaving it on that note.

Dylan hadn't texted yet, which was beyond worrying. Dylan was barely keeping it together and doing a terrible job of acknowledging it.

But the more Liam thought about the way he'd gone about it, the more he regretted it. Dylan hadn't pushed *him* into therapy—he'd been going on his own. He'd been caught by surprise when it turned out he got a lot more out of it than he expected, but he'd been ready to change, too.

Dylan was mired in fear: the accident, and before that, from his life upheaval as he switched schools, and from raised voices and crowds and kids...

Liam hadn't experienced that. Sure, he'd swallowed a hell of a lot of trauma signs—avoidance, hyper-arousal, hell, hyper-sexuality—but he hadn't built his life around this one trauma. He'd sort of unintentionally focused his sex life on it, but at work, he could push it aside. Running into young, drunk guys was the worst it got these days. Liam was bigger and stronger than them now... and he wore a uniform. They listened to him.

"So, I saw my ex again."

That yanked Liam out of his train of thought. He looked up at the barbecue, where Chris was putting burgers on for them. "Yeah? Finally stopped ignoring you?" He chose the sentence carefully to avoid a pronoun. Maybe it was a series of little coincidences, but he couldn't remember Chris using one yet, and he of all people was attuned to that nuance.

"Yeah, uh, this out-of-town trip got in the way." Chris waved it off. "I know, it's still an ex, it's still dumb, but we're gonna give it a shot."

"Cool." Liam smiled. "Well, can't be any worse a pick the second time around. Right?"

"Right." Chris narrowed his eyes and laughed. "Are you insulting my taste?"

Liam nodded seriously. "Definitely."

"Dick," Chris snorted. "See if I pull out my big, beefy burgers for you next time."

"Whoa, I thought we were going somewhere else with that sentence," Liam grinned broadly. "I'm glad I don't get the flat burgers."

Chris grinned back. "Those are the in-law burgers."

"Oooh. Harsh," Liam winced.

"Nah, they deserve it. I mean, this particular set, not that they're *in-laws* yet," Chris hastily added, and the look on his face made Liam laugh.

Liam wanted to ask: *Is it a guy?* But he'd just lost one of his closest relationships—if not *the* closest—in a long time over pushing too hard, too fast.

I guess that's the lesson. Let people go at their pace. Just because he was ready to rush headlong into the fire didn't mean everyone was.

A few seconds later, Chris closed the barbecue lid and looked over at him. "Can you keep something between us?"

Liam's brows rose. "Yeah. What?"

"Uh..." Chris fidgeted, passing the tongs between his hands before tapping them on the plate and setting them down to grab his beer bottle instead. "This ex was a guy."

Liam grinned. "Thought so."

Chris's jaw dropped as he stared at Liam, the beer can halfway to his mouth. He looked mortified. "You *what?*"

Liam took pity on Chris, because he could see him going through it in his head: *did I drop a pronoun? Was it something I said? Did?* He knew that mental spiel. "Not until, like, three days ago when you told me about him. You never once said *she*. I just put two and two together. The others don't know."

"Oh." Chris's shoulders sank with relief as Liam rose to his feet and approached, but he still looked nervous of something.

Liam punched him in the arm, then pulled him in for a quick one-armed hug before stepping back to swig his beer. "Doesn't matter to me, you know that."

"Yeah, I know." Chris looked grateful anyway. He cracked the lid to peek at the burgers.

Liam paused, narrowing his eyes. "You ever told anyone before?"

Chris shook his head.

"Shit, man." Liam felt... honored. "It'll get easier," he promised. "If you keep telling people, that is."

"I might not for a while," Chris admitted, laughing quietly. "It's too... new yet. What we've got. Him and me. I mean, old, but new again now that we've changed, and... yeah. You get what I mean."

Liam's stomach clenched. *Thank God I didn't run around telling everyone about Dylan. Oh, wait. I did.* "Yeah."

"Speaking of which," Chris said, opening the lid to flip the burgers. "You're like a fucking caged tiger. What happened with Dylan? After the accident?"

Liam blew out a quick sigh and ran his nails along the can, scoring it in geometric patterns. "Basically... he's pretty much a wreck right now, 'cause, you know. Trauma. He won't get help. I told him he should, and... uh, kind of pushed him away."

"Right. So, did you apologize yet?"

Liam blinked. "No. He hasn't texted." It was the lamest excuse ever when he said it out loud, and Chris only had to give him a look before he laughed and swallowed a few gulps. "I know. It's more complicated, though."

Chris scrutinized him for a moment. He pointed the tongs at him. "Where's the guy who fights fires?"

"What?" Liam crinkled his nose.

"You're giving up. Don't make the same mistake I did," Chris told him. "That's not the Liam I work with."

"It's different."

"Is it?" Chris left him to think about that one while he turned, grabbed a plate, and took the burgers out.

Liam headed to the picnic table, then fidgeted with his phone. Another notification.

When he opened the app, he stared for a second at the message, not even really registering it. *I never had something good come out of this.* Hooking up could be healthy if he'd gone into it with a healthy attitude. All he'd done to himself was try to hurt himself, over and over. Every message that came in played hell with his emotions, made him think about that incredible sex, the heights of pleasure they'd reached, and the steep fucking fall afterward.

Maybe he'd set himself up to hurt himself with Dylan. Maybe Dylan was using him the same way. But they'd had too many intimate moments for it to be just sex, or just an experiment. Dylan had genuinely cared about him this whole time, and... he cared about Dylan, too.

A lot.

Fuck it, Chris was right. Dylan needed him, and he wasn't even going to try to fight for him?

He swiped out to his home screen, then held his finger on the app.

Deleting this app will also delete its data.

He pressed Delete, then watched his other apps jump up to fill its place. There couldn't be a blank space. Something would always take that spot.

"Burgers are up." Chris dumped his plate in front of him, then grabbed the ketchup. "Want another beer?"

"Yeah." Liam looked over their food at his friend, then pocketed his phone. "Thanks, man."

"Don't mention it."

As Chris headed for the house to grab two more cold ones out of the fridge, Liam made himself draw a deep breath and let it out, forming his plan.

He had Saturday off, and Dylan usually did, too. He'd give him a few more days to cool off, and then he'd go apologize.

Setting up his problems to run from him was no better than running away himself. It was time to man up and face them.

25

DYLAN

"It's gonna be *awesome*, man!"

Rod had downed two Red Bulls before picking Dylan up, but he'd reassured Dylan twice that he hadn't been drinking yet. It didn't stop Dylan from his moment of bitterness that someone jacked up on caffeine could drive, but on anxiety, they could lose their license.

But he was supposed to be forgetting about that tonight.

It was Friday night, which meant parking in Isla Vista, the student neighborhood of Santa Barbara, was nigh-impossible. They were circling the darkened, crowded residential streets to look for parking.

Everyone else here had the same plan as them tonight: drunk students stumbled down the sidewalk solo, in pairs, or in boisterous groups. Dylan's heart was already pounding, but there was something thrilling about this, too.

Maybe Rod was right: exposure therapy *could* help. Liam had gotten to a pretty normal place—they'd even hooked up, before it had all gone wrong, and it sounded like he'd hooked up with enough guys before Dylan. He'd clearly thrown himself in headlong, and he'd never shut down the way Dylan did.

If he could do it, so could Dylan.

He jerked his finger toward an empty spot. "There! Between those two cars."

"Nice spotting, my man!" Rod eased the car into its parking spot with a tricky bit of parallel parking that Dylan had to admire. "And we're off to the races! Relax, dude. Tonight's gonna be a good night!"

Dylan smiled as he climbed out of the car, shoving his hands in his pockets and following Rod down the sidewalk. He wasn't familiar with this area of town, let alone after dark. Isla Vista was smack-dab in the middle of the university campus. From what he'd heard, the huge houses here were often split six, ten, even twenty ways between students to afford the rent stumbling-distance away from the campus.

And, of course, the frat houses were located here. It was to one of them that Rod was taking him. Dylan didn't remember what Greek letters it was, and frankly, he didn't care. He just wanted to get completely smashed and forget the last couple of days... or weeks. He was off that weekend, and he planned to not leave his apartment.

He'd spent Thursday hiding at the clinic and the store. He'd walked to a bus stop down the street to wait for his ride home after his craft store shifts. That way, he didn't have to risk seeing Liam coming or going from his apartment. Most of today, he'd spent on campus with Rod.

Dylan's chest felt like it was breaking open every time he thought about Wednesday, so beyond that first night, he hadn't spared it any thought. Liam still snuck into the gaps between every single other thought he had, but that would fade eventually, he hoped.

"Right!" he said, too loudly. "Which way?"

"Left." Rod squeezed close to him to pass a group of loudly laughing students, grinning at the girls who passed, then steered him around the corner. "Can't miss our house, man. Oh, I'm fucking psyched. I get to move in September. Can't wait to ditch my crappy lease on the place near you —sorry—"

"I'm not offended!" Dylan laughed. "I don't even live in the same complex."

"Yeah, but that whole place is lame. *Isla Vista*. This is where it's at, baby," Rod hollered, earning him cheers from a group drinking in the front yard across the street.

Red plastic cups littered the sidewalk, raised voices all around. Here a party, there a party, everywhere a party— Dylan's head spun around, trying to track them all down.

It seemed like every third house or apartment building along this street had a party in the front yard or visible inside. This was the kind of place people could just crash the closest one.

"This is nuts," he laughed as Rod steered him toward a mansion with Greek letters on the front. His chest was tight, but despite how much his head spun, he kept moving. That was the important thing.

"It's like this every week! Friday and Saturday nights. This is the *place to be*," Rod told him, slapping his back as he pushed him through the gate.

There were already at least a dozen people in the front yard, half of whom cheered at the sight of Rod.

"Rod! Hey, man!"

"Where ya been? About time!"

"The chicks are here! Party's just getting started!" That guy, a broad-chested guy in a hideous orange t-shirt, came around the lawn chairs to slap Rod's back. He stuck out his hand to Dylan. "Jack."

"Dylan." Dylan shook hands, wincing at the stickiness. "Where can I get a drink?"

"You've got your priorities right!" Jack approved with a laugh. "Bar's inside, basement. Beer's on us for prospects. You look like one." He elbowed Dylan and winked. "Tell Blaine I said yours are comped. Make sure you say comped, not free. That's the code word."

Jack says my beers are comped. Fuck it, I'm not rushing, but I'll take it. Dylan grinned at how easily he was taken in, even if he didn't look the part compared to everyone else outside. This was the socks-with-sandals and backward-baseball-cap crowd. "Thanks, man."

Rod accompanied him inside, pointing out the bathroom, the massive living room already half-full of half-drunk girls in short dresses and guys talking loudly and jostling each other around.

This had never been Dylan's scene, but he could blend in for the night. He could put on an act... he couldn't act like Rod, but Liam?

Yeah, Liam could fit in here if he wanted to. He pushed his shoulders back and stood straighter as they clattered downstairs to follow the sound of raised voices to the basement.

"Hey, man!" Again, Rod made the rounds of the room, slapping backs, shaking hands, and introducing Dylan.

Guy after guy, all with the same kinds of names. Ash, Johnson, Brian, Kevin, and two Matts stood between him and the bar, and then he repeated the line he'd memorized and found a red plastic cup of beer being handed to him with a wink.

"Party girls coming through!"

Whoops and cheers accompanied eight girls stumbling downstairs, held up by each other. Dylan noticed they got their beers free, too. He downed his and held out his cup for another, to laughter from the guys nearby.

He could do this.

By the time they made it back upstairs to the living room, he'd downed a couple more beers. The space was filling up with people, and he was okay with that because he was a little tipsy. His anxiety was settling into the back of his mind. He'd forgotten how much drinking helped keep him focused on talking, listening, and staying upright.

He'd met probably thirty people by now, and everyone was cool. He'd expected a few more side-eyes for being so damn... well, camp. It wasn't like he tried, but it just sort of *happened*, especially when he was drunk and not watching the way he shifted onto a hip or wiggled his head when he told a story.

His last attempt at partying had ended disastrously, back in his freshman year. The first time he'd taken freshman year, that was. He'd tried to come to a kegger like this, and he'd wound up melting down in the corner until they called him an ambulance, thinking he was having a heart attack.

He'd almost forgotten *that* detail. Christ, that had been almost the most embarrassing part of his freshman year.

He needed more beer.

Once he got that, Jack was inside. He was making the rounds and talking to all the guys who weren't already brothers. When he reached Dylan they clapped hands like old friends, and then Jack toasted him. "What's your major, dude?"

"Psych."

"Great choice! You'll get a job in ten years," Jack laughed, and Dylan grinned.

"Fuckin' true," Dylan lamented. "BA, MA, blah blah blah." He waved his half-full cup, watching it slosh. "You?"

"Business. I wanna work at my dad's business."

"Cool." Dylan clicked cups with him, then looked around.

Rod was sidling up to a girl near the food table who was giggling at his doubtless terrible jokes, her arm looped around his shoulders. Food sounded good, but not if he had to watch Rod make passes at her.

"If you don't wanna watch that show, there's more food upstairs," Jack told Dylan with a laugh. "Hope you weren't counting on a ride home."

"Not with how much he's planning to drink," Dylan grinned, which earned a laugh and toast from Jack as he moved on.

When Rod's hand went up the girl's skirt and she leaned into him and mouthed at his neck, and then the two of them stumbled off for the basement, Dylan knew he was definitely ditched.

He'd probably been here for an hour without feeling like he was choking and freezing and flying out of his own body, but more groups of friends were arriving now. They crowded the living room and staircase down to the basement. Couples were already forming, and the screaming and laughter from the crowd inside echoed over the music pumping through the place.

But he was okay. For now, he could be here and do this and *not* panic. That was better than he'd ever done in his life.

How many goddamn people were inside?

It was hot, too. Stifling. He was roasting alive in his long-sleeved collared shirt, and rolling up the sleeves only helped so much. Cologne and perfumes clashed in the air, mixed with the scents of sweat and beer. The sour smell of beer only grew stronger after the first beer pong game started.

Dylan needed more beer of his own to deal with this. Before he could head for the basement, though, he heard people yelling about a keg upstairs. A quick check upstairs showed slightly thinner crowds—more like double the crowd he was comfortable with instead of three or four times it.

And there was food! Oh, fuck, yeah. He'd hang out up here for a while.

"Hey! What's your major?"

Dylan lost track of how many beers he'd had, and he was devouring any snack food nearby with a vengeance. The guy who'd talked to him was kinda cute, and according to the loud whispers from one of the brothers nearby, was gay.

Dylan wasn't planning anything with the guy, but they had a friendly kind of fraternal bond just from being surrounded by straight couples sucking face all around.

He was pulled into a conversation at the chips table about the best snacks with Gay Brother—he forgot the guy's name—and he found himself laughing along. Gay Brother had strong opinions about Doritos, and he was hotly debating them with a handsome commerce major from New York and a couple of fine arts students who'd crashed the party.

Then the conversation turned to politics, sports, and TV. Dylan kept up through the TV conversations and the political ones. But at last, he bowed out when they started talking about football or something he knew nothing about.

Liam would have known what it was about. Dylan was pretty awesome tonight. He was doing the world's best job pretending he was confident enough to talk to people. But he wasn't *that* awesome. He couldn't literally suck the knowledge from his inspiration.

It hurt to think about Liam. Why the fuck had he chosen Liam, anyway?

Time for a refill. Dylan stumbled to the bathroom at the end of the upstairs hallway where the keg was tapped.

Once he took a leak, he planned to get yet another refill of the red cup he'd been clutching like his lifeline all evening. Christ, he'd been drinking a lot, but he had to break the seal eventually.

He realized halfway there that he could hardly stand, and there were so many people crushing into the staircase and upstairs landing that he could barely get out.

And he couldn't see any windows from this angle.

It was stupid how fast it came on, the second he noticed it. He'd been upstairs for... God, how long? He had no idea. Hours, maybe. He'd been in the hallway for much of that time, or stumbling between bedrooms talking to friendly guys and girls from frats and sororities whose names he couldn't remember, and pledges, and those who'd just crashed the party. Even the stifling heat and the constant jostling from people around him was tolerable when he was drunk enough.

But now it was all he could do to walk the twenty feet down the hallway, shove his way between a guy in a varsity jacket whispering into some girl's ear and a group of five students who were figuring out how to do a keg stand.

Shit. He was never going to get out of this place alive.

It was an anxiety thought: that was all it was. He knew that much. But why didn't that make it any easier to push out of his brain?

He groped a few times for the door handle to push the door shut. The pipes in the bathroom were exposed, and there were missing tiles in the showers. Only one toilet, but three showers. That was weird.

Windows. He needed fresh air, now. That usually helped— he could gulp some cool air and feel more like himself. Salty, fresh air was the best. This street was near the ocean. He remembered walking into the house and passing... ocean views. Right. Windows. He'd almost forgotten.

He leaned back and slowly scanned the room for them. Fuck. They were at the top of the bathroom wall, way too high up to reach without a chair or something. A look around showed him none of those.

Okay. Take care of his bodily needs, wash his hands, and grab his keys in his pocket to keep himself focused. Then, calmly walk through the yelling, jostling, grinding, dancing hordes and outside. Don't freak out. Don't freeze up. Don't start crying or curl up into a ball or something equally mortifying. Get a taxi. Go home and sleep everything off. Try not to think of Liam.

He could do this.

Dylan only made it through his plan up to grabbing his keys. He was swaying on his feet in front of the door, but he couldn't bring himself to open the door again.

Fuck. Fuck, this was a mistake.

He was never going to make it to the sidewalk outside without completely freaking the fuck out. He was already freezing up, his body shaking. Oh, that was a weird sensation—the room violently spinning around him while his legs twitched and shook under him.

And people were shouting, hollering, singing outside the door—so loud, so *close*, with just one thin wooden door to protect him. There were a couple of other bathrooms, but sooner or later someone was going to want this one.

Dylan leaned hard against the door, blind panic rising in his body until his hands were numb. He could barely feel his face.

And the heat. Fuck, it was hot.

Focus. My phone. I can get it.

Slowly, he wiggled it out of his tight jeans pocket, then brought it closer to his face and further away until he found a point where his eyes could focus.

Slowly, he typed in his password and opened the messages app.

Slowly, he scrolled through his message threads.

Shit. Who the fuck could he ask to pick him up?

Oh, no.

No, it had to be him.

It was sure as fuck not going to be his mother. It couldn't be Vee or Gary, obviously. Why didn't he have more fucking friends?

Oh, right. Because he was a loser who did *this* at parties—called for help.

His hands shaking, Dylan's heart rose into his throat. He didn't have a choice. There was only one person he trusted to come for him, and he had to pray he was right.

He thanked God for autocorrect as he took his time typing a letter at a time to get it right.

I'm in isla. I need you. I'm sorry.

Dylan hit Send and his breath hitched in his throat, his chest tight again. Liam had walked out the door with his shoulders down. He hadn't been angry, Dylan reminded himself. Maybe he had a—*yes!*

He slowly read the response, and he could have cried.

What happened? Where? I'll come.

Dylan kissed his phone and looked around for the name of the fraternity. They had it on fucking flags everywhere. Sure enough, there was one.

He texted back the name one letter at a time without processing the whole thing, hoping autocorrect hadn't mangled it. Before he could say anything else, someone knocked on the door and yelled something about needing water.

It took all his focus to open the door and stumble into the bedroom next door, which only had, like, a dozen people. Then he raised his phone almost to his face again, his hands trembling.

Thank God everyone was too busy to notice him. Some people were already sprawled out on the floor, others on chairs or the bed.

Frat party. Went wrong. Can't breathe.

He sank onto the floor and knelt there, leaning against the wall as he tried to breathe. Whatever cologne was in here, it was horrible.

On my way.

There was shouting from somewhere nearby, but he couldn't process it. Too loud. Too much noise. Too close.

There was an unholy screeching from somewhere—everywhere—and the volume of the crowd on this floor only went up. Someone turned up the music to drown it out.

"This happens when there's too many people! Heat sensors!" someone was shouting over them while someone else tried to jab at the "off" button.

Dylan's vision of the hallway outside was blurry, and he could barely look up when someone else burst into the room, laughing obnoxiously. "The kitchen's on fire!"

It clicked slowly—way too slowly.

It wasn't his eyes. It was smoke in the hallway.

Some people were shoving and jostling for the stairs and panicking, screaming at each other to move. Some people just stood there and laughed their asses off. Some people danced like they didn't care.

And Dylan watched himself slumped in the corner, gripping his phone so hard his knuckles were white in a desperate attempt to make himself *feel* his own body. Like that would mean he suddenly had control of it again.

Liam was on his way.

26

LIAM

It took Liam a minute to find parking along a side street near the frat house. He'd looked it up on Google the moment Dylan had texted him the name. Isla wasn't his territory, but he still knew it reasonably well. He liked to be prepared to provide backup in other crews' areas.

His chest was tight and he walked fast around the obnoxious students clutching cups of beer and trying to avoid house party raids. The last place he'd expected to find himself was around them, but as he reminded himself, none of them looked twice at him. And he had one major advantage: he was sober.

Among the shouts and laughter coming from all around, raised voices from a couple of guys sprinting away from the frat house caught his attention.

"Man, someone better call 911!"

"No fucking way! You know how many of us are freshmen? The cops are, like, two streets away!"

Liam's heart pounded, but he stepped in the way of one of them. "Man, what's going on?"

"Fire, dude! Someone was smoking on the back deck. Get

out of here before the cops show up," the guy answered, shoving around him to keep running.

There were more people running, now, and shouts. Screams. And the smell of smoke.

Liam stepped aside to let a cluster of friends shove each other through the front yard, then strode toward the house. Music still pumped out of the open windows, but the shrill shrieks of fire alarms were piercing the night. He could still see some silhouettes upstairs, and smoke drifted out of the upstairs windows.

All the windows open would only give the fire a shit-ton of oxygen. That much smoke from inside, if it was supposed to be the back porch on fire? The structure was compromised, no doubt about it. Every second was critical now.

Some people—the sober-looking ones—were on their cellphones, amidst the hordes taking videos. Good, 911 knew.

Liam knew it could be ten minutes before the engines showed up—especially if they had to get a rig through drunken, frantic crowds. He heard police sirens. Cops would be here any minute now for crowd control, and he prayed to God they focused on that and not ID'ing drunk teens, but that wouldn't help get people out.

There were a group of guys in the front doorway, laughing hysterically, almost doubling over as they clutched each other. They were taking a selfie, ignoring the people trying to shove past them.

Fuck. Okay. Drunk idiots.

A structural fire in a frat house packed full of drunk teens and young guys, some of whom probably weren't taking it seriously?

And, worst of all, Dylan was inside. His last text: *I can't breathe.* No answer to Liam's follow-up, sent from the first red light he'd hit.

E. DAVIES

A small part of him hoped that maybe Dylan wasn't inside. Maybe he was in the drunk tank, or sobering up with a burrito at Freebirds. Maybe he'd gone home already. But no, that wasn't Dylan. If he'd been able to text again, he would have. He was having another of his panic attacks, and with that kind of crowd? No fucking wonder. Even Liam would have one.

When he shoved his way onto the porch, pushing people toward the front gate, the guys pushed him back off the porch.

"Get the fuck *out*. That's a *fire*, you idiots," Liam snapped, drawing himself up to his full height. He was pissed.

"You get out," the guy snarled, shoving Liam again. He was clearly far past sober. Probably drugs. Just drunk, he'd have fallen over already. His buddies still kept the doorway blocked, and some people were pulling open downstairs windows to climb out from the living room.

Dylan was trapped in there, and these assholes wouldn't let him inside. Without the protection of his uniform and his buddies at his back, he felt half-sick with rage and fear. And his hands were shaking.

Drunken frat boys. Of course. His trigger. Now was *not* the moment.

Last therapy appointment, though, he'd suddenly understood: a part of him he'd desperately ignored for so, so many years was deeply afraid. All it—all *he*—wanted to do was protect Liam. That was why he started shaking when someone found him appealing, before he could take control of the situation.

But that part of Liam was gone now. He wasn't the scared little boy from all those years ago. He was probably ten years older than these guys, and he could deadlift any of them—he'd have to if they'd been inside.

Take control.

186

That brought his mind back to the moment. Inside. How many people were still in there?

He scanned the crowd again, then turned back to the guy facing off with him and jerked his thumb aside. Without the uniform, he'd try a different approach. "You got your selfie. Cops are here. Whatever you're on, they're gonna want a word."

That broke through. The guy's eyes widened, his urge to fight vanishing. "Fuck. Come on, guys!"

He and his buddies took off around the side, jumping the fence into the backyard as another flood of people—everyone who'd been stuck behind them—came pouring out of the building, half of them hysterically sobbing.

The smoke behind them was thickly billowing. This wasn't just a pan on fire. Nobody was laughing anymore. Anyone bursting out of the house was terrified.

Liam took a quick step back, glancing up to take in the place. Three stories, at least, and Dylan could be anywhere. At least there wouldn't be a crowd of idiots around him to save, too.

Christ knew how long the place had been burning, or what had even started the fire. Nobody he stopped on the way out knew.

And nobody knew Dylan's name, until one guy did a double-take. "Scrawny guy, yea-high?" He gestured around Dylan's height. "Psych major?"

Liam almost jumped at him. "Yes! Where is he?"

"Upstairs," the guy told him, his syllables slurred as he stumbled for the fence and his friends tried to get him to move further away. "There's a couple people... there. He was in a corner. Looked sick."

There were only stragglers stumbling out now, and the cops were approaching. Liam had to get in before they tried to keep him out. He couldn't afford to wait for the rig to show up and the guys to vet him. The longer he waited, the less chance...

No. Liam was going to focus on this job.

Thank God he was wearing a cotton t-shirt and jeans. They weren't turnout gear, but synthetic materials melted fast. He didn't see flames yet—mostly smoke. He had a chance. There were too many variables to predict when this would go from dangerous to insane, but he couldn't wait any longer.

One breath to save him. Two breaths and you're the second patient.

Superheated air flashed the lungs, and then he wouldn't be breathing oxygen—or probably anything anymore. Liam gulped as much air into his lungs as he could and pushed into the heat of the house. His steps were quick but measured, his eyes narrowed against the dark smoke as he scanned the living room.

Clear.

He moved toward the back, crouching and squinting under the rush of smoke. Nobody in the kitchen, but he could see flames on the back deck. He couldn't get there without gear, but he could guess they were licking up the siding. If the Charlie side—the back of the building—had ignited, that explained the smoke from the top floor.

Noise—someone was stumbling up the basement stairs, coughing and sputtering. They couldn't make it all the way up. Smoke inhalation, probably. Asphyxiation was the leading killer. Liam was instantly focused. Dylan or not, that civilian was his next priority.

It wasn't Dylan. The girl wore a short denim skirt with a tank top, but she looked uninjured. She was just running out of energy.

Liam took a few steps down the stairs, light without his gear, and hauled her up over his shoulder with a grunt of exertion. As he turned, he carefully let some of the air out of his lungs. Holding carbon dioxide in, as much as lack of oxygen, weakened the body. She coughed and clung tight, her hands fisting in his shirt.

A few more strides and he was over the threshold with her, and there were cops helping her off him. The engine was parked outside, and the guys were running hose toward the house and walking the perimeter. The crowd had been pushed back beyond the fence now.

He recognized Charlie striding over to do first aid, but everyone else was in full gear already, so he couldn't tell who they were.

Charlie had a moment of shock at the sight of him. "Liam?"

Liam jerked his head in a quick nod to Charlie. He didn't have time to explain what he was doing here. He crouched by the girl and took her hand. "Charlie's got you now. Was there anyone else downstairs?"

She shook her head.

He scanned her face intently, looking for any doubt. "Are you *sure*?"

"Positive. Basement's e-empty aside from the bar. And I was hid-hiding there—" She started coughing and couldn't get words out.

Liam let go and rose. He clapped Charlie on the shoulder as he headed for the truck. Dylan was definitely upstairs, and if he was going to make it, he needed spare turnout gear. He hoped the guys carried it on this apparatus.

"Whoa. Liam. What are you doing here?" Chief Williams was there, hauling open a compartment and looking cool and calm as always. Seeing him was no surprise at a scene as big as this.

"Long story." Liam reached past him to grab full-length boots and pants first.

Chief Williams let him do it but put his hand on his shoulder. "You're sure?"

"I'm sober and rested," Liam swore, praying Chief Williams wouldn't realize he had an ulterior motive. "Let me help. At least until backup's here. It's a big place. At least three stories at the rear." This was the kind of fire that happened a handful of times in a career. It could wind up a multiple-fatality fire if they didn't get inside now.

Chief Williams nodded once. "Were you inside?"

"Just now. Girl says she's sure the basement's clear." They'd be checking anyway. Not worth the risk she was wrong. "At least one person upstairs. There's a back deck, but I couldn't check it." Liam's training carried him through as he explained what he did know, pulling the jacket on and grabbing a hood.

"Go with Cal," Chief Williams told him once he was dressed.

Liam relaxed as he grabbed a set of irons. Cal was solid. He trusted him by his side. "Yes, sir."

Two more guys were stumbling outside, walking on their own but supported by Cal. The radio buzzed in his ear, telling him that the basement was clear.

Liam breathed easier in his gear, though his lungs were still itching from the smoke from his first entry. The smoke was thicker as he followed Cal back inside, scanning the room once more for survivors. No way could he have made it in now.

"We have reports of victims trapped on the second floor," Liam told Cal. "All intoxicated, probably."

"The first floor's clear," Cal answered. "We can't stay in here long, though. The back wall's compromised."

He signaled upstairs and Liam nodded, following on his heels.

The worst part was taking the stairs one at a time when he

knew Dylan was upstairs, but it was protocol. They couldn't slip and fall in gear this heavy.

Sure enough, the back wall was on fire. As he'd guessed, flames had licked through the window, igniting the windowsill. Flames were already eating away at the wooden structure. They could hear the guys on the radio still, setting up lines around the place. It looked like it had started on the back deck, but the back wall was the priority now.

"Unit three, victim on the floor by the window," Cal suddenly said. There was someone—too tall and dark to be Dylan—near the windowsill, unconscious. "I've got this one."

Cal hefted him over his shoulder and headed for the stairs while Liam checked out the other rooms along the Charlie side. He even yanked open the closets. People did stupid shit when they were scared and drunk.

Nobody.

He looked over his shoulder to check that his exit route was still safe. "Nobody left on B or C," he reported over the radio, already heading for the A-side—the side overlooking the street. A little hope rose in his chest that Dylan wasn't in here. Maybe he was somewhere else. Maybe that guy was wrong, and he'd gotten out before the fire had started. Maybe he'd missed him in the front yard.

Liam nearly missed it: something in the corner. No, someone. The second his eyes landed on the slender body and the floral shirt, he knew who it was.

"Victim unconscious near the window. My exit route's clear, but not for long. We'll need a rescue ladder to check D."

"Multiple victims by a window in D. Unit three, can you see anyone from there?"

"No, the hallway turns ninety degrees," Liam answered as he crouched by Dylan. "I'm in the corner room of A and D, heading for the stairs."

191

He spared a second of thought to pray that Dylan was just unconscious from smoke inhalation. He was far enough away from the flames that his lungs hadn't been burned, unless he had ended up here after running.

Dylan was light on his shoulder as he hoisted him, and limp in his arms. He didn't look burned, his clothes intact for now. The soot and particulates from the fire were going to ruin his shirt by the time he was out.

He was gonna be pissed about that.

Focusing on that kept Liam distracted from the *what ifs*: what if he didn't make it? What if he'd only been here to distract himself from their... breakup, or fight, or whatever you'd call that? What if he'd never pushed Dylan into finalizing the transfer, and he'd never been here?

"Unit three. Sir, the fire's maybe three feet away from the top of the stairs. The top landing will be compromised soon," he reported back over the radio. It already creaked under him, and he winced. The risk of falling through a floor in full gear— or with a victim—was bad.

There was no time for distractions. In the roughest technical lingo, this place was about to get wet. Water meant steam. Steam could burn bare skin faster than naked flame.

Dylan had to get out, now.

He kept his body between the flames licking through the air and Dylan, moving as fast as he dared to get him down the stairs. When he got there, he could barely see through the smoke on the first floor now.

Just as he'd been trained, he thought back to recall the way in, looking to the ground to pick out the shapes of doorways and reversing his path.

"Rescue ladder on Delta. Three civilians trying to climb out the window."

The open air was cooler even through his gear. The relief

wasn't from being able to see, or the sudden temperature drop, or even his own safety, though.

The EMTs were crowding around as he shifted Dylan from his shoulder to the stretcher, then stepped back. He recognized two of them, but not the third.

They were checking his airway and breathing, but Liam couldn't stay with Dylan. There were other civilians in danger, and their first backup engine was only arriving now. This blaze was going to be bad. It was eating through the back of the building like it was paper—his fire science course told him that something was wrong with the construction, the way it was moving.

Dylan was safe with the EMTs. His life was in their hands now. Liam's job was to get others to them, if anyone was left inside.

"Victim trapped on the back deck."

Liam looked at Cal. Cal responded to the call, and they moved as one. They hadn't worked together every day beyond Liam's initial tour of the houses in the area, but they'd trained together before. They both knew how bad this was going to be.

"Be careful," Chief Williams told them. "We'll protect you, but we can't hold it for long. Be ready to get out."

"Yes, sir," Liam answered automatically, picking up the pace with Cal.

They both knew there was a point when they'd be called out. Liam didn't believe in a higher power most days, but on days like today, he prayed to anyone that was listening that it wasn't until after they found their civilian, and that they weren't going after a body.

The deck was a wraparound style and low—not a second-story deck, thankfully. There were no safe routes in, but there were calculated risks, and he and Cal decided at the same moment which one to take.

Four or five guys were already back there, covering them with lines. The smoke was billowing furiously now that the flames were being attacked, and the heat was rising to almost uncomfortable points.

Walking through flame always gave Liam an adrenaline rush. As he pierced the veil to reach the smoldering part of the deck where their victim lay, something jigged into place. There was one huge difference he hadn't considered between this and his other potentially self-destructive habit.

This was something that changed others' lives, or saved them. He was good in bed, but not good enough to say he rocked anyone's world the way he did when he carried them out of a burning building.

The way the guy's limbs were askew made Liam wince. Must have run from the last few rooms Liam hadn't been able to check and straight into the fire, then panicked and jumped. The part of the deck where he'd landed was still burning, so his skin was blistered, but when Liam crouched by him, he saw chest movement. He was still alive... for now. Possible neck and spinal injuries meant their rescue was going to be far from ideal, but life came over limb.

"Victim on the back deck, possible head, neck, spinal injuries," Liam radioed. "Are we covered?" Water blasting behind them sent a hiss of steam that made Liam wince. They had to move now.

Liam moved as one with Cal to grab the guy's wrists and shirt, hauling him into a sitting position before grabbing his belt.

"Move fast and you've got an exit route," someone told them on the radio. "Same way you came in. Structure's compromised, though. Go now."

They looped his arms around their shoulders, and Liam ignored the pain starting to sear his back. He'd had to turn his back on the fire—one of their many "rule one"s—to do this.

Cal counted. "One, two, *three.*" They stood together, hoisting their victim up. Liam's training meant it was nearly automatic to move with Cal through the dampened flames until they were stumbling onto the lawn beyond. They kept moving with him until they were nearly in the side yard and well clear of the building.

The deck collapsed, embers flying in another rush of flames.

When Liam peered down the side yard toward the command center, he counted only one ambulance, and a horde of police cars. Three engines now, with a fourth in sight. He was positive there'd been two ambulances before. Was Dylan in one of them?

Screaming pierced the air, and it wasn't coming from the sidewalk. A cold shiver ran down Liam's spine. Shit. At least one victim was still inside. It was a miracle they were still conscious. That, or a curse. They'd know which soon.

"Unit three." That was them. "Backup on side Delta. We've got a second rescue ladder."

Liam tamped down his fear. *Dylan was still breathing. I think.* He was fast on ladders. He was needed.

"On our way."

"Liam, Cal, you've done enough."

There were fresh guys here now, and backups from the county. The fire raged steadily now, but not out of control. According to their checks and all reports, there was nobody left inside. It was just a matter of suppressing the flames and smoke now, keeping the buildings next door safe.

Liam knew Chief Williams was right.

"Especially you, Liam. Christ. What were you doing here?" Chief Williams frowned as Liam leaned on the truck, pulling his helmet and hood off for blessed fresh air.

He was soaked in sweat, and his back hurt. He had to get someone to look at that, make sure it wasn't burned. Now that the victims were all in the hospital or had left without needing medical attention, they'd have someone free to do that.

"The first guy I pulled out," Liam answered, still out of breath. "That was Dylan."

He left his turnout gear where he'd found it. It felt like he was naked without the thick layers covering his body.

Chief Williams stared for a few long seconds. Then he nodded. "You didn't have to keep working." There was admonition in there, too—protocol said he shouldn't have.

But fuck protocol. He'd done what needed to be done.

"Of course I did," Liam shook his head. "I gotta get checked out and then see where they took him."

"They might not tell you," Chief Williams said, his voice strangely gentle.

Liam gritted his teeth as he turned to head for the ambulance. "Then I'll track him down."

Another call came in on the radio—Chief Williams was needed. He paused and nodded once to Liam.

Liam was sure he wasn't imagining the respect there. It made his chest swell as he nodded back. He strode for the ambulance.

The sounds of roaring, crackling flame never quite left the back of his mind, but far worse were the screams. He was shaking lightly as he sat down, ate something sugary the paramedics gave him, and stripped his soaked cotton shirt off for them to look at his back.

He knew Pat, the guy who came over to have a look at him.

It *was* a burn—minor, all things considered, but a bitch to heal. He hated sleeping on his front.

"One thing," he said as he breathed his relief at the cool ointment one of the EMTs was spreading down his back. "Oh, God, that's good. Thanks, Pat. One of your patients earlier. Dylan Waters. You know which one I mean? The first guy I brought out."

"Yeah. We found his wallet. I know him. You can put your shirt on, but you know the drill." Pat moved around to stand in front of him.

"You took him to the hospital?"

"Yes."

"Which one?"

"Liam..."

"I know." Liam winced as he pulled the damp shirt back on, trying to sit straight so it clung a little less to his skin. "But I... I know him. He doesn't have anyone else." Pat still watched him levelly and Liam growled under his breath. "Fucking HIPAA. I'm his... we were dating, okay? SBCH?"

Finally, Pat's shoulders and his expression softened. He glanced left and right, then leaned in. "If it were, I wouldn't be able to tell you."

Liam let out a slow breath. "Thank you."

"Oh, don't thank me. I didn't say anything."

It was so late that it was early, the sky a few shades lighter than when Liam had come here. He was exhausted, sweat-soaked, and aching, but he couldn't go home yet.

There was someone who needed to go home much more than him.

27

DYLAN

"I'm... allowed to go?"

"Yes, honey." The nurse by Dylan's bed smiled patiently at him as he repeated it dumbly. He was sober now—or most of the way there. But he was exhausted, sleep tugging at his eyelids and beckoning him.

He had to get home. How was he going to get home? God, the taxi fare was gonna kill him.

No, it won't, dumbass. Not like a fire. He almost laughed. There was a bit of perspective for him. Two near-misses later, why he was still saying that?

Liam didn't come for me.

It was the thought he'd been trying his hardest to avoid—the one that made his chest clench every time. Dylan tried to ignore the weight in his chest that overpowered even the itch in his lungs and his raw throat.

He'd woken up alone, surrounded by sterile white and two nurses, an oxygen mask strapped to his face. The only thing that had kept him from panicking was the pure oxygen. He could use a tank of that at home.

Smoke inhalation, they'd said. But there were no fluids or dangerous particulates. Drink water, avoid cigarette smoke, and take the inhaler they'd prescribed if he needed it. Come back if anything worsened. It would take time before his lungs fully recovered, but eventually he'd be able to breathe deeply again.

And given how often he breathed deeply to keep his anxiety down, he didn't know how that was going to work. Dealing with the doctor and nurses alone was easy enough when there were only a couple of them, but crowds? Whenever he made it to class again... *if* he went back to class... would be the real test.

He changed from the hospital gown into his street clothes again, wincing at the smells of smoke and beer. Gross.

When he pulled back the curtain, looking around to try to find his way out, the nurse approached again, a set of blue doors swinging behind her. Lindsey, he thought her name was. "There's someone waiting for you."

"There... is? Mom?" Dylan questioned. The nurses had said they'd called his emergency number while he was unconscious—no answer. No surprise. Maybe she'd woken up and come to find him. God, what time was it, even? He pulled his phone out, then grimaced at it. Dead. Hopefully from a flat battery, and not... fire.

"No. You gave your emergency contact as your boyfriend. We couldn't let him in, because we couldn't verify his identity..."

She was talking, but Dylan tuned out for a second. When had he done that? *Oh yeah. When they woke me up and frisked me for insurance.* He hadn't even known what he was thinking —just that Liam might have figured out where he ended up, and might answer since his mom hadn't.

"He's here?"

"Yes. He's waiting just out there."

She barely pointed at the doors where she'd just come from before Dylan was walking—no, running.

And straight into Liam's folded arms and scowl.

He only had a second of fear about what that meant—*oh shit I said he was my boyfriend, is he pissed off?*—before Liam's arms were around him, his face tucked into Dylan's neck.

"Shit. Oh, God, I didn't know if you'd made it until they told me *just now*, and it's been hours..." Liam's voice was hoarse, and he smelled like sweat and smoke. Not just smoke, but something chemical and metal.

Dylan coughed hoarsely and turned his face away to catch his breath, but he squeezed Liam as tight as he dared despite Liam's quiet yelp. "You came."

"Of course." Liam was rubbing his back now, those broad hands cupping his shoulder blades and running down his spine gently. "Are you hurt?"

"Smoke inhalation."

"Thank God. I mean, not that you had that, but... of everything..."

Why did Liam smell like smoke? He wasn't working today, was he? But as Dylan pulled back and took in Liam's appearance—sweaty, exhausted, but pale with relief—it clicked into place.

"Shit. You went in?"

Before Liam could answer, Lindsey cleared her throat behind them. "You're Liam, then? Dylan's..." She rustled papers. "...boyfriend? You're here to take him home?"

Dylan winced and looked at Liam to apologize.

But, to Dylan's surprise, Liam just smiled softly over Dylan's shoulder, his arm snaking around Dylan's waist. "I am." Liam didn't clarify which of the three questions he was answering, until he looked at Dylan. "You ready to go home?"

Dylan leaned into that broad chest, his shoulders sagging with relief. "Yes, please."

The next few minutes passed in a fog. Dylan signed papers and thanked the receptionist and stumbled out to Liam's car with him. The whole time, Liam had a hand on him—his shoulder or his back.

"Sorry I told them that," Dylan mumbled when they were both in the car. "I didn't think Mom would come, so I fibbed a little. In case you were here. So you could see me. If you wanted to."

Liam paused before he started the car. He drew a deep breath, making Dylan envy him for a moment, then reached over to take his hand. "It doesn't have to be a lie."

Oh. Dylan's heart soared as he looked over at Liam, already smiling. "You mean, you want to date me...? After all that?"

Liam was smiling, too. "Yeah," he nodded once, firmly. "If you want me, I'm... yours."

If he wanted him? Dylan almost laughed that it was even a question. "Oh, God, yes."

"All right," Liam laughed. The stress lines in his face had disappeared as he watched Dylan, but he still looked exhausted.

"You didn't sleep, either? Were you on the scene?"

Liam nodded and started up the car, and Dylan was too tired to be nervous about him pulling out of the parking lot.

Dylan caught his breath. "Fuck. Did you... I mean, was I...?"

"I was the one who found you."

Dylan could only imagine what that had been like. He shuddered. No wonder Liam was so certain of his answer a minute ago. "I'm sorry."

"No, I'm sorry. But let's save the apologies until we get

home," Liam smiled. "My place or yours? Ah, you probably want—"

"Yours."

Liam looked startled as he looked over, and then he relaxed into another smile. "Okay. Mine it is."

Dylan closed his eyes for a moment, and Liam was lifting him into his arms. He nestled into Liam's chest, not thinking about how weird it was that he was picking him up while driving until he cracked his eyes open. He caught a glimpse of the dawn light filtering along the shopfronts of State Street, and the familiar green doors of the craft shop and Liam's apartment.

He was home.

28

DYLAN

Daytime meant nothing to Dylan by the time he woke. He had no idea what hour it was, and he found he didn't care.

Especially because Liam's arm was wrapped around him, and his face was tucked into Liam's strong chest.

They both smelled fresh and clean—Liam had been right to make them shower before bed, despite Dylan grumbling about it. Dylan barely remembered the shower Liam had guided him into, and scrubbing himself off, swaying on his feet from exhaustion until Liam toweled them both off and bundled them into bed.

He liked being naked, though, his body pressing into Liam's. The cotton sheets were cool against his bare skin, but the heat of Liam against him was making heat rise in his own body.

He was the one who found me. The thought made Dylan tear up. His breathing quickened until Liam's arm gradually tightened around him.

His boyfriend shifted, pressing his lips into Dylan's hair and pulling his face into his shoulder. "Shh. What's wrong?"

"I... just..." Dylan breathed out, blinking his eyes rapidly. His lashes tickled bare, tanned skin. "Thank you."

He wasn't ashamed that he'd had to be rescued. He'd hit rock bottom, after all. But there had been someone there to save him, and he would never forget that. It was okay to be saved sometimes. He'd be happy to take a break from being saved from near-death by Liam dragging him out of harm's way, but maybe... he could let Liam drag him out of his comfort zone, too, and find help.

Maybe.

"It's my job," Liam murmured, his thumb tracing Dylan's spine to the back of his neck. "And if it weren't, I'd still have done it. I..." Then he stopped and cleared his throat.

Dylan swallowed back the tears and laughed gently. "Yeah. Course you'd say that. That's why I love you."

It fell from his lips so damn easily considering he'd never stopped and thought about it, never sat down to weigh it up: *reasons I might love him, reasons it might be just a crush.* But perhaps that was why it felt so natural.

He just knew.

"I love you, too, Dylan. I was about to say that," Liam laughed gently, squeezing him.

Dylan's smile was broad as he pressed close. "I only worry about your job, but I can't imagine you doing anything else."

Liam smiled gently. "I have more chance of..." Then his eyes widened and he shut his mouth.

"What?" Dylan laughed.

"Getting... into a car accident." If he didn't look so sheepish, Dylan would wonder if he was making fun of him, but Liam looked mortified. "Sorry."

Dylan's answering laugh bubbled from his chest. Liam joined in the laugh a moment later. "I'll keep that in mind,"

Dylan teased. Once their giggles subsided, Dylan nuzzled into Liam's neck. "Are you... okay if I do this?"

"Oh, baby, I'm just fine with it," Liam whispered. He was still smiling lightly. "It's different when it's someone I know. I might get a little shaky just from... habit... but it's just that. A reflex. I realized in all of that who I am, and it's not the scared little boy I once was."

Dylan nodded. He had the strangest feeling he knew what Liam meant, even if he was miles behind him now. "If we're being honest... I wish I could be that... chill."

"You can be," Liam promised, running a hand through his hair. "If you want to be, and if things work out with therapy. And even if they don't, I'd take you exactly as you are now. You don't *need* to change. I just want you to do what's best for you."

Christ. How the hell had he landed a man this perfect? Dylan was tearing up again as he pressed his lips against Liam's chest, letting Liam rock their bodies together for a moment to soothe him.

Then he noticed his cock sliding against Liam's with each rock, and that Liam wasn't soft. He wasn't exactly hard yet, but Liam had noticed him. It made him giggle.

"Mmm?" Liam chuckled quietly.

"You like sleeping next to me all *naked*?" Dylan whispered for dramatic effect, squirming closer to grind against him.

Liam laughed quietly. "I really, *really* do. I didn't want to be a perv, though."

Dylan grinned. "I've had a long fucking week. I would love nothing better than your cock in me this morning... afternoon... whenever it is."

"Oh my God, yes, please," Liam moaned. "Can we do it again? Only this time without the sadness and the fights? I promise not to be stupid."

"So do I," Dylan laughed, running his hand down to Liam's

E. DAVIES

ass to squeeze it and appreciate the fitness and muscles and general shape of it.

Liam was touching him now, too, as he rolled Dylan onto his back and braced his arms above his head.

And they were kissing, Dylan's lips meeting Liam's in a burst of pleasurable heat. They kissed deeply and slowly, Liam's body rubbing along Dylan's as Dylan ran his hands up Liam's sides, grabbing his head to hold him still when he needed to suck his lip or slide their tongues against each other's.

He was desperate for it by the time Liam dipped his fingers into his mouth and then between Dylan's thighs, rocking his fingers inside slowly. "Yes! Oh, fuck," Dylan hissed, curling his toes into the bed as his lover's weight pinned him to the bed.

It lulled the anxiety about what they'd say or do this time after sex that lingered in the back of his mind. Instead, he focused only on the moment.

Liam's hard cock was rubbing between his thighs as Liam pulled his fingers out.

Dylan reached between them to lick his palm, then reached between Liam's legs to slide his wet hand up and down the shaft, stroking and squeezing the solid weight. "Did you... while we were...?"

"No. I didn't hook up. I wanted to, the part of me I'm working on, but... I didn't want to," Liam said softly, straightforward.

Dylan's face split in another smile up at his gorgeous lover. *See? You're getting so much better.* He was proud of him. But he'd have lots of time for that later. "Me neither. And I want you like this again."

"Okay," Liam whispered simply, letting Dylan guide him to the entrance.

Dylan pulled his hand away to let Liam take over, grabbing

his back instead. He didn't miss the wince that crossed Liam's face. "Are you okay?"

"I'm a little burned," Liam admitted. "Shoulders would be better. Or my ass," he winked.

Dylan laughed, gliding his touch down Liam's sides to his ass instead. "Sorry. Are you okay?"

"I'm just fine," Liam murmured, his voice soothing Dylan's momentary anxiety.

Then, he was pressing inside, splitting Dylan open and filling him up. Fuck, he was *there* again, inside Dylan, in a way Dylan hadn't dared imagine for himself.

This second time, it meant so much more.

"I'm *more* than fine," Liam added, his voice a low moan as he pressed his lips to Dylan's neck. "This is so... God."

"I know," Dylan whispered, his body shivering with pleasure at the hardness in him, linking them together. "I love you," he whispered, just to hear it out loud again.

"I..." Liam pushed as deep as he could go, then thrust again, "fucking..." Dylan was grinning by this point, but let him finish the sentence with his third thrust. "*Love you.*"

Dylan kissed Liam hard. Their bodies were sliding as one now, Liam's fingers locking with Dylan's above his head before they let go, touching each other as if to confirm they were here.

They were really here, together. Neither of them felt whole, but neither was ashamed. Dylan loved Liam exactly the way he was, and from Liam's words... it was impossible for anyone to feel unloved with a man who looked at him like Liam did.

Liam treasured him.

Dylan moaned and let go of one of Liam's hands to haul him in by the back of his head, kissing him hard while Liam thrust harder. The mattress creaked, and the sounds and smells of sex were utterly intoxicating.

More than that, he kept wanting to smile, even laugh. It was so strange. That had been one of the worst moments in his life just last night, and now...

Fuck, had he *ever* felt happier?

Dylan resisted the urge to hug Liam so he didn't touch his back, but he wrapped an arm around his shoulders. Liam's lips were on his neck again, kissing to his shoulder, then down his collarbone, which made him shudder and moan in approval. He rolled his head to the side to let Liam take all he wanted; Liam did just that and gave back more.

His arousal sparked through his whole body, every inch of his skin sensitive against Liam's. He could feel Liam's nipples against his own, and Liam's thighs, and his flat stomach with those washboard abs. He could feel every press of Liam's lips to his ear, neck, throat, or lips.

Dylan felt every second of it, and he'd never been more alive.

His cock was aching for more touch than Liam's stomach, but Liam already had it covered. His hand slowly ran down Dylan's body, making Dylan arch off the bed, until that broad, hard palm wrapped around his shaft. His other hand let go of Dylan's to touch his chest instead, and Dylan burned with pleasure.

"Fuck," Dylan moaned. "Yes, please, Liam. Yes..."

Liam squeezed and stroked, and Dylan almost disappeared into bliss. Liam pushed deep inside him with each thrust, grinding against the sensitive spot inside him at *just* the right angle, and Dylan's whole body flinched and trembled. He was so close to the edge, so desperate to come for him, but also to have Liam come *in* him.

He was his now, and he wanted to feel it.

"I'm gonna—I'm never gonna last," Dylan warned, his voice already breathy. The slightest brush of Liam's hand to his nipple, cheek, or side did him in. "Oh, my God. Yes, Liam…"

Dylan could feel the end coming as Liam's lips pressed his for one more hot, filthy kiss, his tongue darting out to slide against Dylan's. At the same time, Liam jerked his hand along Dylan's erection harder, making him throb with pure desire.

The second his other fingertips brushed Dylan's nipple, his body overloaded with sensitivity and spilled over the plateau's edge. He was falling into need, into pleasure, into *love*.

And he was coming, clenching around Liam and crying out hoarsely as he spilled into ecstatic oblivion. "Liam…!" was all Dylan managed. He couldn't breathe, but this time it was because he was glowing with indescribable bliss that crawled from his core to the tips of his fingers.

Liam was gasping softly into Dylan's ear, making a little noise with every thrust of his hips. His voice was so quiet, but so goddamn *sexy*. "Yes, I—Dylan, I'm… oh, God. I love you. This is… I'm gonna…"

"Come for me," Dylan moaned, wrapping his arms tightly around Liam's shoulders and pressing their lips together. He kissed Liam until Liam came in a flood of warmth, Liam's body slamming into his as he gasped for breath against Dylan's lips.

And then he kissed him a little longer, just for good measure.

When Liam finally slid out of Dylan, all Dylan could do was laugh breathlessly. "That… Wow."

"Wow," Liam echoed, his face tucked into Dylan's neck. One broad hand on Dylan's hip while the other slid up the bed to lock with Dylan's again. When he lifted his head again, Dylan made sure to peck his lips several more times for good measure.

They kissed quietly, except when one of them chuckled or pulled back for breath. There was nothing *funny*, exactly, but the joy of this moment, of *being* together, and of being here together, flooded them both in equal measure.

"No lectures this time," Liam whispered against Dylan's lips at last, and Dylan giggled softly.

"No kicking you out."

"Good. I don't know where I'd go if you kick me out of my own place," Liam pouted.

Dylan laughed again and closed his eyes. "God. I'm sorry I did that. You were trying to help."

"No, I was being dumb," Liam told him. He was still blanketing him, and Dylan tightened his arms around Liam to keep him there. "I thought... Oh, it doesn't matter."

Dylan opened his eyes to peek at Liam. "That you were broken?" The surprise and vulnerability on Liam's face took him a moment to register, and when he did, he kissed Liam gently. "Me, too."

Liam breathed out quietly. "Yeah," he admitted then. "But you're not broken. That's not you. I mean, it's a part, but not *all* of you. It's not what you *are*. You think that pain is most of you, with bits of you around it, but it's the other way around." His voice was soft but steady. "I did a lot of thinking while I was waiting for you in the ER. There's so much of you, and I love every bit of you, including the pain. Please, let me be here for you. Don't you dare push me away again."

"Christ." Dylan had to close his eyes to blink away the tears. Nobody had ever told him... anything close to that. "I won't, as long as you don't do it to me. I want you to push me now, however scared I get. I'm ready to deal with it and get help, and... not just to keep my license, but... 'cause I feel like I'm worth it now."

In all the speeches about loving yourself before someone could love you, nobody had ever said it could be the other way around—that having someone love the broken bits of Dylan could make him love those bits, too, and want to glue them together the best he could.

He wasn't comparing himself against perfection anymore. Even Liam wasn't perfect. But he saw the way Liam tried, and it made him want to try, too... for his own sake.

The next words made Dylan close his eyes for a long minute, just to let them sink in.

"You're worth the world."

EPILOGUE

LIAM

"Sorry, we have to duck out early." Liam bundled his needles and yarn together, ready to take upstairs.

"See? They start dating and forget about the rest of us." That was George, a retired cop who liked to knit baby sweaters for his grandkids. His wife had taught him two years ago, and now they did it together, except when he was here at the therapy circle.

Velma grinned. "I keep losing my employee, too. He spends half an hour every morning staring at the door, hoping Liam will be knitting downstairs with him today."

"Not... *entirely* true," Dylan defended himself, turning red as he stood up. "We have friends coming over is all."

"Ohhh. That hurts," Ben teased. He was a freshman in university, and he'd started off dealing with trauma from a car accident.

Liam knew almost all their stories now; he considered them friends just as much as Dylan did. He offered an apologetic smile. "A friend who doesn't knit."

"Is not a friend at all," Vee clicked her tongue. "But go on, before your firemen friends catch you."

Liam laughed. Chris knew by now that he knitted, and although he'd spent about a month making fun of him for it, he envied the sweater Liam had made for himself—with copious help from Dylan, of course. Liam had told Chris he could learn to knit and make one for his damn self.

"He's got some new fling he wants us to vet," Dylan shrugged. "Who are we to argue?"

Liam laughed gently. Chris was going through a phase of trying on men, trying to figure out what and who he liked. His ex had quickly turned out not to be the answer to that question.

"Bye, guys. See you next week," Liam promised, his hand on Dylan's back as he steered him through the side door and up the stairs.

As soon as they were inside, Dylan took over cooking while Liam set the table. As always, Liam smiled at the set of knitted heart coasters he'd given Dylan as their one-month anniversary present. They only had a couple of minutes until Chris and his date showed up.

"What do you think he'll be like?"

"This one?" Dylan giggled. "I don't know. He hasn't dated an otter yet."

"Oooh. Young, rugged, nice scruff? Sure. I'll put my bet on... uh..." Liam stuck out his lip in thought, and Dylan kissed it on the way by. He laughed. "A twink."

"As twinky as me?"

Liam winked. "I doubt it."

Dylan clicked his tongue and flicked a dish towel at him. "Chop up the onion and stop sassing me."

"Yes, sir," Liam said, but he sidled up behind Dylan, slid his arms around his waist, and kissed the top of his head instead.

Dylan leaned back into him, stirring the sauce in the pan

with a smile. Apparently, he'd gotten his cooking skills from his mom. They'd seen each other a few times in the last couple of months since the fire, but things were... cool, at best.

Liam admired how Dylan was handling it. She was neglectful at best, even if she tried to care... in slightly wrong ways. She'd called Dylan from his doorstep the afternoon after the fire, waiting to deliver several casseroles and a lasagna. Dylan had talked to her about why she'd reported him, and again, it was caring, but slightly misguided.

Instead of trying to change her, Dylan was working on himself, and Liam couldn't be more proud. Since getting his license back and another cheap car so he could drive himself to class again, Dylan's confidence had skyrocketed. Despite having the shittiest couple of months of his life, Dylan had said several times that they were the best, because he'd met *him*. It always made Liam blush to the tips of his ears.

Liam just held Dylan, reflecting on how goddamn glad he was not to be in that rat race of dating anymore. He had his man, and Dylan was perfect no matter what.

Dylan was the piece to his puzzle that he hadn't even known he was missing. There were rough days at work, and sometimes there were arguments over who should do the dishes, but Liam never once complained about it. Living, sleeping, staying in or going out with Dylan was worth it.

There was a knock on the door, and Liam heaved a sigh. "I guess I have to get that."

"Mm." Dylan twisted in his hold to peck his lips. "We can cuddle later, once we see..." he lowered his voice to a whisper, "if Chris's taste has gotten any better."

Liam laughed richly and squeezed Dylan once more before he headed for the door. "Bet it hasn't."

"Bet you're right."

"I'm always right."

Dylan snorted ungracefully and ladled sauce into the other pan. "I'll let that one go."

Liam's last thought, totally unbidden, made him smile even though he kept it to himself.

And I'll never let you go.

AFTERWORD

Dear reader,

Thank you for reading *Afterburn*. No matter the cause, PTSD can be debilitating and it's so often misunderstood. It means a lot to be able to write about it from the heart.

Chris's story is up next in *Afterglow*, and it's also a hard read. Take care of yourself, and please seek support if you need to.

Thank you to my Facebook group, Ed's Petals, for embracing and uplifting this series, along with all my other books. This was such a hard series to write! If it touches you, please consider leaving a review so others can find it, too.

Make sure you sign up for my newsletter to hear about: exclusive free short stories and sales; new releases in ebook, audio, and print; preorder alerts; sneak peeks at upcoming books; event appearances; and other exciting news as it happens!

I also have a reader group on Facebook if you want to chat about your favorite parts of *Afterburn*, see cute bee photos and good news stories, and keep on top of my upcoming releases with a whole bunch of lovely readers: facebook.com/groups/edavies

Last but not least: always be you!

~Ed

NEXT IN AFTER

AFTERGLOW

Everyone has limits, but sometimes they hurt.

Loud-mouthed firefighter Chris Black is newly out and should be having the time of his life. But booty calls from his ex-boyfriend and coming home to an empty house have his optimistic spirits low. When he answers Ash's cry for help, Chris finds his total opposite—and everything he wants.x

Ash never expected to wake up to a gorgeous stranger fighting to save him. It's just the start of a long road, and at last, he isn't walking it alone. Without a safe home to return to, Chris offers Ash his guest room—and more. Ash is drawn to his savior, but he's not going to be used ever again.

It's the perfect arrangement at first. Ash gets the help he needs to adjust to his new limits, and Chris gets a friendly face at home. But where there's smoke, there's fire. Can they clear the air in time, or will their new love fizzle out?

Afterglow is the second book in the After series, which explores mental health challenges with gentle humor and heart while hunky firefighters turn up the heat. It can be enjoyed on its own, and promises a happily-ever-after.

ABOUT THE AUTHOR

E. Davies grew up moving constantly, which taught him what people have in common, the ways relationships are formed, and the dangers of "miscellaneous" boxes. As a young gay author, Ed prefers to tell feel-good stories that are brimming with hope.

He writes full-time, goes on long nature walks, tries to fill his passport, drinks piña coladas on the beach, flees from cute guys, coos over fuzzy animals (especially bees), and is liable to tilt his head and click his tongue if you don't use your turn signal.

facebook.com/edaviesbooks

twitter.com/edaviesauthor

instagram.com/thisboyisstrange

bookbub.com/authors/e-davies

Brooklyn Boys

Electric Sunshine

Live Wire

Boiling Point

F-Word

Flaunt

Freak

Faux

Forever

After

Afterburn

Afterglow

Aftermath

Men of Hidden Creek

Shelter

Adore

Miracle

Redemption

Audiobooks

You can see all my books available in audio here:
edaviesbooks.com/audiobooks

9 781912 245062